KEEPING SECRETS

"Maybe," Lisa said, "just maybe, Tessa and Veronica actually . . . like each other."

Carole gasped. "No way," she said quickly. "Tessa is a member of The Saddle Club. And Veronica is, well . . ."

"Pure evil?" Stevie suggested helpfully.

Carole laughed wryly. "Well, I was going to say Veronica is Veronica," she said. "But either way you look at it, it just doesn't make sense."

"Should we just come right out and ask Tessa about it?" Carole said.

"I don't know," Lisa said. "Maybe we should wait a few days and see what happens."

"Are you sure?" Stevie sounded worried. "Don't forget, last time we tried to keep a secret from Tessa—"

"I know." Lisa cut her off. "But this is different. We're not hiding anything from her. If anything, she's the one hiding something from us."

THE SADDLE CLUB

ENGLISH RIDER

BONNIE BRYANT

A SKYLARK BOOK
NEW YORK · TORONTO · LONDON · SYDNEY · AUCKLAND

RL 5, 009–012

ENGLISH RIDER

A Bantam Skylark Book / July 1998

ISBN 0-553-48630-6

Published simultaneously in the United States and Canada.

Bantam Books are published by Bantam Books, a division of Bantam Doubleday Dell
Publishing Group, Inc. Its trademark, consisting of the words "Bantam Books" and
the portrayal of a rooster, is Registered in U.S. Patent and Trademark Office and in
other countries. Marca Registrada. Bantam Books, 1540 Broadway, New York, New
York 10036.

PRINTED IN THE UNITED STATES OF AMERICA

OPM   0 9 8 7 6 5 4 3 2 1

*I would like to express my special thanks
to Catherine Hapka for her help
in the writing of this book.*

"THAT WAS FUN," Lisa Atwood said contentedly. She leaned forward to give the horse she was riding, a tall, lively chestnut gelding named Derby, an appreciative pat on the withers.

One of Lisa's best friends, Stevie Lake, nodded. "After a trail ride like that, aren't you *extra* glad that Max didn't ban us from Pine Hollow?" she teased.

Their other best friend, Carole Hanson, shuddered. "Don't even joke about that." Her horse, Starlight, fell a few steps behind as the riders left a wooded trail and entered a sunny meadow. Carole urged him forward a little faster. "We've had some pretty close calls since Max put us on probation."

"It's just lucky Veronica didn't manage to convince

him that we were behind that trick last night." This time the speaker had a distinctly British accent. The speaker was Lady Theresa, known to her friends as Tessa, who was visiting from England. Tessa was referring to a trick the four girls had played the day before on Veronica di-Angelo, a fellow rider at Pine Hollow Stables. Veronica's family had a lot of money, and that made her think she was more important than everyone else. Although she was a better-than-average rider, the other girls often thought that the snobbish Veronica cared more about owning an expensive horse and wearing fancy clothes than she did about horses or riding.

Lisa thought about that now as she and her friends trotted across the meadow on their way back to the stable. She couldn't understand Veronica's attitude at all. She herself was interested in just about everything about horses, but the clothes she wore ranked near the bottom of the list.

Lisa's love of horses and riding was shared wholeheartedly by Carole and Stevie. That was why the three girls had started The Saddle Club, which had only two rules: All members had to be willing to help one another out, and they had to be horse-crazy. Since starting The Saddle Club, Lisa, Carole, and Stevie had invited a number of other friends to join as out-of-town members. Some of these members, including Stevie's boyfriend, Phil, who lived nearby, came to Pine Hollow frequently. Others, including Tessa, lived too far away to visit very often. But where they lived didn't make any difference. The important thing was that all of them cared as much about their friendship as they did about horses and riding.

Lisa glanced around at the scenery as the four friends rode slowly across the broad, white-fenced pastures behind Pine Hollow Stables. Taking in the lush, rolling Virginia landscape, the familiar scents of horses and clean leather, and the perfect summer day, Lisa couldn't imagine anything she would rather be doing than completing a leisurely trail ride with her friends—except maybe starting another one.

Still, The Saddle Club had recently come very close to losing their riding privileges for a good long time. And as usual when there was trouble at Pine Hollow, Veronica had been involved.

It had all started on the last day of school, when Veronica had secretly arranged for Stevie to receive an award for best-dressed boy. The bogus prize, presented at a school assembly, had been an ugly plaid necktie arranged in a fancy gold frame.

Stevie had a wild and wacky sense of humor, and she could take a good joke as well as she could dish one out. Normally she might have appreciated the humor of the prank and let it pass. But she and Veronica had always gotten along about as well as cats and dogs, and Stevie drew the line at being humiliated by her archenemy in front of their entire school. She had vowed to get her revenge at any cost.

As the girls paused to open a gate between fields, Stevie was thinking about that very topic. "I still can't believe we attacked the Penningtons by mistake," she muttered as she rode through into the next field. She pulled her horse, Belle, to a halt to wait for Lisa to close the gate again.

Stevie's revenge scheme had backfired. She, Carole, and Lisa had hidden in Pine Hollow's loft and tried to pelt Veronica with water balloons. But they had fired too soon, accidentally soaking Max Regnery, the owner of Pine Hollow and the girls' riding instructor, along with a wealthy older woman named Mrs. Pennington and her preppy teenage grandson, Miles. The Penningtons appeared to have forgiven The Saddle Club, but Max hadn't been so willing to let them off the hook.

"No kidding." Carole rolled her eyes. "If it hadn't been for that, Max wouldn't have threatened to suspend us from the stable. And we wouldn't be forced to let Veronica do and say whatever she wants without even trying to do anything about it."

"I still feel awful about all that," Tessa said mournfully. "If I weren't here, Veronica couldn't be nasty to me. And if she couldn't be nasty to me, she wouldn't have such an easy way to get your goat. *And* you wouldn't have to worry so much about doing something to make Max turn your probation into suspension." Veronica and Tessa had first met when Max, The Saddle Club, and Veronica had visited England for an international Pony Club rally. At first

Veronica had been awed by Tessa's title and her distant kinship to the queen of England. But once Tessa became friends with The Saddle Club, Veronica's admiration had quickly faded.

Stevie shrugged. "Don't be silly, Tessa," she said. "It was when we reminded Max that you were coming to visit that he decided to put us on probation instead of just kicking us out for a couple of weeks."

"Stevie's right," Lisa added. "Besides, Veronica's obnoxious personality is her own fault, nobody else's. You can't help it if she doesn't like you."

Stevie nodded emphatically. "In fact, you should probably take it as a compliment."

Carole grinned and moved Starlight a little closer to Topside, the horse Tessa was riding. "They're right, you know," she told Tessa. "I think Max thought you might be a good influence on us while you were here. Little did he know that you would be the mastermind behind last night."

The evening before, the girls had finally managed to get back at Veronica. Tessa had told the Pine Hollow riding class about a long-ago event known as the Midnight Steeplechase, when British cavalry officers had run an informal cross-country race after dinner wearing nightclothes over their uniforms. The students had decided to run the same kind of race themselves. But when The Saddle Club handed out maps, Veronica's had been different from everybody else's. Instead of riding through the woods to the real finish line, Veronica had galloped off in the opposite direction, ending up at the Penningtons' home. Upon arrival, she had found Miles Pennington and half a dozen of his teenage friends waiting for her. The fact that Veronica was wearing ridiculous pajamas and a silly nightcap over her riding clothes—and the fact that she had a huge crush on Miles—had only made the whole scene funnier as far as The Saddle Club was concerned.

"The best part of last night was that Veronica couldn't prove it was us who sent her the wrong way, since the boys ripped up her map," Lisa said.

"I know." Tessa sighed. "Max did seem a bit suspicious, though. I never would have forgiven myself if our prank had cost you your riding privileges."

"Well, we never would have forgiven ourselves if we'd let Veronica get away with making your visit miserable," Stevie declared loyally.

Carole nodded. "True," she said. "By making Tessa miserable, she was making us all miserable. And she knew it."

"I just hope she's given up now," Lisa said worriedly. "I mean, that little prank last night doesn't even begin to make up for all the grief Veronica has caused us—"

"Hear, hear," Stevie put in wryly.

"—but I'm sure she's not going to see it that way," Lisa continued. "Especially if she thinks we've cost her her chance with Miles."

"I see what you mean." Stevie nodded and paused for a

6

moment as she gently pulled Belle back into line. The curious mare was trying to wander off to explore an intriguing patch of weeds. "Even if Veronica can't convince Max that we arranged that prank," Stevie said, "she knows very well that we did it. I hope she doesn't get even meaner now."

"Me too." Tessa frowned. "As I said, I'd never forgive myself if I got you suspended from riding."

Lisa could tell that Tessa was really worried about the whole situation. That wasn't fair, since it wasn't her fault. But Lisa suspected that it would be next to impossible to convince her of that right now. "Enough about Veronica," she said briskly. "We should be talking about more interesting topics. Like the point-to-point."

The Willow Creek Country Club was sponsoring an event called a point-to-point to raise money for charity. Lisa's mother and Mrs. diAngelo were both on the committee in charge of the fund-raiser. A point-to-point was a sort of amateur steeplechasing event. It would consist of an entire day of jumping races, including one limited to young riders like the members of The Saddle Club.

"If we're going to talk about the point-to-point, we're going to have to talk about Veronica again," Stevie said. "After all, she's the one who fixed things so that Tessa can't ride in the junior hurdle."

Lisa frowned, realizing that Stevie was right. In all the excitement of the previous night's prank, she'd almost forgotten that Veronica had arranged for Tessa to be a fence judge for the race, thereby eliminating her as a competitor. No matter how hard they thought about it, The Saddle Club couldn't seem to find a solution to that predicament.

"Don't worry about me," Tessa put in quickly. "I'm re-signed to being a judge, really. It's not worth getting you in trouble."

"Maybe you're right." Carole shrugged and smiled. "Anyway, we'll still have fun together watching the other races and stuff."

"Right." Tessa looked relieved. "And I'll be right there to cheer all of you on in your race." She glanced over at Lisa. "You and Derby seem to be getting on famously."

Lisa could tell that Tessa was trying to change the subject. She decided to let her. "We are," she said, leaning over once again to pat her horse. "He's been wonderful." Lisa normally rode a Pine Hollow stable horse named Prancer, and she loved the beautiful Thor-oughbred mare. However, Prancer had an inherited weakness in her leg that had ended her earlier career as a racehorse. Max and Lisa had agreed that it would be too dangerous for the mare to race in the point-to-point. Even though it was just an informal race, run-ning and jumping at full speed might put too much strain on her bad leg. Instead, Lisa planned to ride Derby, a recent arrival at Pine Hollow. She had been practicing on the big gelding all week.

"Come on," Carole said. "Starlight still feels pretty lively. Why don't we canter the rest of the way home?"

Her friends didn't bother to answer. All three of them immediately signaled to their horses, and all three horses immediately broke into a swift canter. Once again, Carole and Starlight had to hurry to catch up.

"DID YOU HEAR the news?" Stevie asked, walking into the tack room an hour later.

Carole, Lisa, and Tessa looked up. All three of them had already made their horses comfortable, and now they were busy cleaning the tack they had used on their trail ride. One of Max's strictest rules was that his riders had to help out with stable chores. For one thing, it kept expenses down. For another, it taught the riders that riding didn't begin and end with sitting in the saddle. A lot of work went into running a stable and caring for horses, from mucking out stalls to mixing feed and cleaning tack. Some students—including Veronica—grumbled about all the work. But The Saddle Club never minded, even the part about cleaning tack. Sitting together in the cozy leather-and-soap-scented tack room gave them the perfect opportunity to hold nice long Saddle Club meetings.

"What news?" Carole asked, leaning over to pick up a container of metal polish.

Stevie set Belle's saddle on an empty rack and grabbed some saddle soap out of the bucket near the door. "I just

9

ran into Mrs. Pennington and Miles," she said. "They were coming in to talk to Max, and Mrs. Pennington looked pretty excited, so of course I couldn't resist asking her what was going on—"

Her friends laughed. Stevie was famous for never being able to resist trying to find out what was going on. Her parents liked to say that Stevie was twice as curious as any cat and three times less shy about showing it.

"Anyway," Stevie went on, ignoring her friends' laughter, "Mrs. Pennington said that the rest of her carriage-driving stuff just arrived."

"Really?" Carole looked interested. Mrs. Pennington had been a talented show jumper when she was younger. These days her arthritis kept her out of the saddle, but it didn't keep her away from horses. She was deeply involved in a whole new equine sport, competitive driving. The week before, she had given a very interesting talk and demonstration to Pine Hollow's Pony Club meeting. Her matched Cleveland Bays, Hodge and Podge, were staying at Pine Hollow while the old stable on the Penningtons' property was being repaired. Mrs. Pennington had hitched the two large geldings to Max's pony cart for the demonstration, since her own vehicles hadn't yet arrived at her new home.

Stevie nodded as she buffed her saddle. "If we hurry up and finish here, we can go find out more. She and Miles are with Hodge and Podge right now."

"You mean you didn't get all the details?" Carole asked in surprise.

Tessa looked worried. "I hope you're not still feeling awkward talking to her because of what happened." For a while after the water balloon incident, Stevie, Carole, and Lisa had done their best to stay away from Mrs. Pennington and her grandson.

"Oh, no, it's nothing like that." Stevie waved one hand, almost upsetting the saddle soap, which she had balanced precariously on the saddle rack. She gave her friends a sheepish look. "It's just that Max came along and shooed me away before I could ask any questions. He was muttering something about filthy tack . . ."

"Say no more," Carole said, nodding wisely.

Stevie sighed. "It really stinks to have Max mad at us," she said. "I can't believe he's holding a grudge for this long."

"But Stevie," Lisa pointed out logically, "Max always grumbles at us about cleaning our tack right away."

"But it was the *way* he grumbled," Stevie insisted. "It was so . . . so *cold*. Not the friendly way he usually does it."

Carole smiled at that. As far as she could tell, Max never sounded particularly friendly when he was trying to get his riders to do their work. Still, she thought she knew what Stevie meant. Max had been really angry about the water balloon incident, and he still didn't seem to be over

11

it. Carole felt terrible about that, and she knew her friends did, too. Max was one of The Saddle Club's favorite people, and usually the feeling was mutual. She hoped they could regain his trust and respect soon. Until they did, their situation was like being on probation twice over—probation regarding their riding privileges, and probation regarding their friendship with Max.

"I'm just about finished." Tessa stood to return Topside's bridle to its spot on the tack room wall. "Give me that bridle, Stevie, and we'll be out of here twice as fast."

Soon after that, all the girls' tack was sparkling clean. They put it away, then headed toward the large box stalls where Hodge and Podge were staying.

When they arrived, they found that the big bays already had a visitor. Veronica was leaning into Podge's stall. From where they were standing, the Saddle Club girls could see a hand holding a brush and grooming the gelding's body, but they couldn't see the rest of the groomer. "He's such an adorable horse," Veronica was crooning, stroking Podge's broad head.

Stevie rolled her eyes. "Guess who's still sucking up to the new rich boy in town?" she whispered to her friends sarcastically.

"Are you sure it's Miles?" Carole whispered back with a giggle. "Maybe Veronica's secretly in love with Mrs. Pennington."

"Shhh!" Lisa cautioned her friends, shooting a worried look forward. Veronica knew all about The Saddle Club's probation, and she had been doing her best to provoke them into violating it. Lisa knew that the snobby girl would love nothing more than to see The Saddle Club barred from riding for a couple of weeks.

Hodge, who was stabled across the aisle from his brother, had come to the front of his stall to watch The Saddle Club's approach. Luckily, Veronica didn't seem to have heard them coming. She was leaning even farther into Podge's stall to talk to Miles. "You're so good with these horses, Miles," she said admiringly. "You must work with them a lot."

"Actually, Hodge and Podge are Grandmother's babies," Miles said. "Grandmother only lets me groom them when her arthritis is really acting up. Besides, she thinks I don't have enough to do since our second team is still in Pennsylvania. Most of the time I work with them."

"Well, you really know what you're doing," Veronica cooed. "And you have such strong hands!"

Stevie pretended to gag. Carole elbowed her in the ribs.

"Maybe we should come back later," Tessa murmured.

This time Veronica heard them. She turned around and saw The Saddle Club standing in the aisle.

Carole braced herself for Veronica's usual obnoxious comments. After the events of the previous evening, she was sure Veronica would be positively furious at all of them—especially Tessa. But something very surprising happened. Veronica smiled!

"Oh, hello," she said.

Carole gulped, not sure how to respond. She glanced at Lisa. Lisa was looking over at Stevie. Stevie was just staring at Veronica in astonishment.

Veronica wasn't looking at any of them. She was directing her smile straight at Tessa. "Hold on a second, okay?" she said. "I need to talk to you."

"Uh-oh," Carole muttered. But she still felt confused. Veronica's voice didn't sound threatening at all. In fact, it sounded—could it be?—*friendly*!

Veronica leaned into Podge's stall again. "I'll see you later, Miles," she called. "Thanks so much for telling me more about Cleveland Bays. I really learned a lot."

"Sure, anytime," Miles called back from inside the stall.

Veronica turned, and Carole caught a glimpse of her self-satisfied smile. She could guess what was going on— Veronica was trying to make Miles forget what had happened at the midnight steeplechase. And she obviously thought she was succeeding.

Veronica hurried toward The Saddle Club. "Listen, Tessa," she said. "I was thinking about something this morning."

"Uh, yes?" Tessa said uncertainly.

"I really think we got off on the wrong foot last week." Veronica still wasn't looking at the other members of The Saddle Club. "I'm afraid I wasn't quite as welcoming as I

14

should have been. I feel kind of bad about it—especially since you're a visitor to my country and everything."

Stevie let out a strangled snort. Carole elbowed her in the ribs again.

Veronica ignored them. "Anyway, I was thinking we should try to start over and forget about the past. I mean, it would be a shame to let a few little misunderstandings keep us from being friends." She shrugged and smiled. "You know, since we probably have a lot in common and everything."

Tessa looked slightly stunned. But her good manners took over. "Why, certainly, Veronica," she said politely. "That's very nice of you."

As she watched the whole scene, Stevie had to bite her lip to keep from saying something sarcastic. She had no idea what was going on, but she was definitely suspicious. Since when was Veronica so forgiving and friendly? Was she still hoping to wheedle her way into an invitation to a royal garden party? Or was she up to something even sneakier?

"Oh, good." Veronica took a step closer to Tessa. "I'm so glad you feel that way. And I have a great idea. I was just about to head home—why don't you join me for a spot of tea?"

"Oh!" This time Tessa looked pleased. "Thank you so much. That would be lovely." She turned to her friends. "Do you mind? I'm sure I'll be back in plenty of time for our sleepover." The four girls were planning to stay at Lisa's house that night.

For the first time, Veronica glanced at Stevie, Carole, and Lisa. "Oh," she said flatly. "Um, I would invite you all, but I really think Tessa and I need a chance to get to know each other. You know, one on one."

Stevie didn't bother to respond. "Hey, Tessa?" she said instead, grabbing her friend's arm. "Can we see you for a second? Alone?"

"Certainly." Tessa smiled apologetically at Veronica. "Would you excuse us?"

"Sure," Veronica replied generously. She started down the hall. "I'll meet you in the locker room in a few minutes, okay?"

Moments later The Saddle Club was huddled in a corner of Starlight's stall. "Are you crazy?" Stevie whispered. "You can't go to Veronica's house! It's got to be a trick!"

Lisa glanced over the stall door to make sure Veronica wasn't eavesdropping. "For once, Stevie's not just being paranoid," she agreed. "Veronica is up to something. You can count on it."

"I don't know . . . ," Tessa said uncertainly. "She looked so sincere." She shrugged. "And if she is being sincere, maybe there's some hope for peace for the rest of my visit. That would be a relief, wouldn't it?"

"I guess so," Carole said. "But only *if* she's sincere. Which she isn't. Veronica is never nice for no reason."

Tessa still looked confused, but before she could

16

say anything else, the girls heard Veronica calling her name.

"I'd better go," Tessa whispered to her friends. "Don't worry—it will be all right. If she's up to something, I'll figure it out soon enough. And if she's not . . ." She shrugged again, looking hopeful. Then she led the way out of the stall.

"Oh, there you are," Veronica said when she spotted them. "Sorry to interrupt your little meeting or whatever. But I just thought of something, Tessa—I'd love for you to meet our daytime maid, Julie." She smiled. "She's from England, too. I'm sure she'd love to chat with you about all the news from back home. But we have to hurry. Her shift ends in half an hour, and we don't want to miss her."

"All right," Tessa said. "I'm ready." She paused just long enough to give her friends one last hopeful look. "Don't worry," she whispered. "It will be fine." Then she turned and hurried off after Veronica.

Stevie watched her go. "Well, that proves it," she told her friends.

"What do you mean?" Lisa leaned against the stable wall.

"Veronica is definitely up to something," Stevie said grimly. "And it must be something big. Why else would Princess Veronica even *think* about talking to a lowly maid?"

STEVIE LOOKED AT her watch. "How long does it take to drink a lousy cup of tea, anyway?" she grumbled.

Carole smiled weakly. "Don't you mean a 'spot' of tea?"

Stevie merely rolled her eyes in response. It was later that afternoon, and she, Carole, and Lisa were sitting around the Atwoods' kitchen table waiting for Tessa to return from her tea date with Veronica.

"Do you think we should really be worried?" Lisa glanced at the digital clock on the microwave. "She's been gone for hours. Maybe Veronica drugged her tea and shipped her back to England."

Carole laughed. "Now you're starting to sound like Stevie," she teased.

Stevie snorted. "Not hardly," she said haughtily. "*I*

would have wondered if maybe Veronica knocked her out with a poison dart and shipped her to Zimbabwe. Or possibly Iceland."

At that moment the sound of the front door slamming rang through the house. "Maybe that's her," Carole said hopefully.

The three friends hopped up and hurried into the front hall. But instead of Tessa, they found a very harried-looking Mrs. Atwood standing there.

"Hi, Mom," Lisa said. "How was your committee meeting?"

"Frantic," Mrs. Atwood replied breathlessly. "I can't believe the point-to-point is in less than a week. There's still so much to do! I just don't know how it's all going to get done. When we agreed to do all the work ourselves rather than contracting it out, I just never realized—"

Lisa glanced at her friends and bit back a sigh. "It's okay, Mom," she said. "We'll help. What do you need us to do?"

AN HOUR LATER Lisa stopped typing and stretched her fingers to get rid of a cramp. "Ugh," she said, leaning back in her chair. She, Carole, and Stevie were scattered through the living room, working hard on the various projects Mrs. Atwood had assigned them. "You know, I'll be glad when the point-to-point gets here. And not just because I'm looking forward to it."

Carole grinned. "I know," she said. "Your mom has

turned us into real workhorses lately, hasn't she?" This wasn't the first time The Saddle Club had stepped in to help with the fund-raiser. Mrs. Atwood had had them making phone calls, drawing up signs, and doing other work all week.

Stevie, sprawled on the floor, looked up from coloring in a picture of a hot dog on her handmade refreshments sign. "Still, it will all be worth it," she reminded the others. "The point-to-point is going to be awesome."

Carole nodded. "I know. I can't wait. Although I am a little nervous about the junior hurdle race."

"Oh, come on." Lisa grinned. "You know you'll do great. You always do." Carole was generally considered the best young rider at Pine Hollow.

"I've never ridden in anything like it before," Carole reminded her friends. "Neither has Starlight. This isn't just a jumping contest. And it isn't just a race. It's both."

"I know," Stevie said eagerly. "Isn't it great?"

"I wonder how many riders will be in our race?" Carole went on thoughtfully. In a way, the junior hurdle sounded very exciting. But it also sounded a tiny bit scary. "I hope there aren't too many. I heard Max say something about limiting the number in each race to make things safer." The country club committee had asked Max to be one of their expert advisers for the point-to-point, and The Saddle Club knew he was taking the responsibility seriously.

Lisa scanned one of the scribbled lists she'd been typing into the computer. "The entry list is right here," she reported. "As of right now there are ten people entered in the junior hurdle, including us. That shouldn't be too bad."

Carole nodded. "It should be just enough to make things exciting without making the field too crowded."

"Of course, it would be even better if there were eleven people entered," Stevie muttered.

Lisa knew that Stevie was thinking about Tessa. That reminded her to check her watch again. It was almost dinnertime. "I wonder what's keeping Tessa?"

"Who knows?" Stevie said, grabbing a purple pen to start coloring in her sketch of a can of grape soda. "I can't imagine anyone spending this much time with Veronica and living to tell the tale."

"Well, I'm beginning to think your theory was right, Stevie," Carole said. "Or was it your theory, Lisa? Whoever thought Veronica was going to drug Tessa's tea and send her back to England."

"I don't know," Stevie mused. "That sounds like an awful lot of work, and you know how Veronica hates to work. I think she'd be more likely to order her chauffeur to drop Tessa off in the middle of the woods, miles from civilization. With no shoes."

Lisa laughed, but despite all the jokes she was starting to feel a twinge of real concern. It was getting late, and it wasn't like Tessa to keep them waiting so long without even a phone call. "Maybe we should call Veronica's house," she suggested. "You know, just to check . . ."

Just then they heard a car outside, and Stevie jumped to her feet. "That must be her," she said. She grinned wickedly. "Unless it's Veronica with the ransom note."

The three girls hurried into the front hall just in time to see Tessa letting herself in. "Oh, hello," she greeted them brightly. "What are you lot up to?"

"Waiting for you," Stevie replied bluntly. "We were beginning to think that Veronica must have fed you to her dogs. Or maybe tossed you into the dungeon."

Tessa laughed. "Nothing like that," she assured Stevie with a playful wink. "Quite the contrary, actually. Veronica couldn't have been lovelier. I had a marvelous time at her home."

Carole noticed something shiny glinting on the collar of Tessa's shirt. "What's that?" She leaned forward for a better look. "I don't remember you wearing a pin earlier."

Tessa glanced down and smiled. "I was just about to tell you," she said. "On our way here, Veronica and I stopped off at that lovely tack shop at the mall and bought matching stock pins. That's why I was a bit late getting home."

Carole, Stevie, and Lisa were still peering at the slender gold pin when Mrs. Atwood came bustling into the room. Tessa greeted her and repeated her explanation. "I hope I haven't held up your supper," she finished politely. "I lost all track of the time."

"Oh, no, not at all," Mrs. Atwood assured her. She examined the stock pin. "My, but this is beautiful," she said. "Veronica diAngelo has such wonderful taste, doesn't she?"

"Her taste in people certainly is improving," Carole muttered to Stevie and Lisa. "Or she's getting better at pretending."

The telephone rang. "Oh dear. That will be Agnes calling about the catering . . ." With that, Mrs. Atwood rushed off toward the kitchen.

Lisa turned to Tessa as the four girls wandered into the living room. "Um, listen, Tessa," she said hesitantly. Tessa seemed so happy and cheerful that she hated to say anything negative. Still, she knew she had to do it. "I realize you don't know Veronica very well."

"I feel I know her quite a bit better after this afternoon," Tessa said with a smile. "Though not as well as you all know her, naturally."

"Naturally," Stevie agreed, flopping down onto the couch. "So I think what Lisa's trying to say is, you've got to be careful. Veronica is a rotten sneak."

Tessa raised an eyebrow in surprise. "I know Veronica can be . . . well, difficult at times," she said. "And she's certainly been unpleasant to me in the past. But she really seems to be making a sincere effort to be nice now."

"But that's just the point," Stevie insisted. She leaned forward and stared at Tessa earnestly. "She's *never* nice. I mean, she's only nice if she wants something. Or if she's trying to pull something over on someone. Or—"

"All right, Stevie." Tessa sounded a tiny bit annoyed. "I hear what you're saying. But what *I'm* saying is that I don't want to cause trouble for no apparent reason. If Veronica wants to be friendly to me, I'm perfectly willing to be friendly to her. After all, it's not as if she's trying to turn me against you or anything like that. She didn't so much as mention any of you all afternoon."

Carole was more than a little surprised to hear that. Making fun of The Saddle Club was one of Veronica's favorite activities.

It was obvious that Tessa was ready to drop the subject, but Carole could tell that Stevie and Lisa weren't. And she understood why, because she felt exactly the same way. Tessa needed to be warned, and they all needed to work together to figure out what Veronica was up to.

"Tessa, listen to me for a second—" she began.

At that moment Mrs. Atwood bustled back into the room. "It was Agnes from the refreshments committee, just as I thought," she chirped. "The arrangements for the catering are running smoothly."

"That's good," Carole said politely. She hoped Mrs. Atwood would leave them alone so that they could talk to Tessa. They had to make her understand how devious Veronica could be. They had to make her see that there was no point in being polite to her. It would only backfire.

Unfortunately, Mrs. Atwood seemed to have no intention of leaving. She sat down on the couch beside Stevie and smiled at Tessa. "Tessa, dear, I was about to ask you when the phone rang—where did you say you and Veronica got those lovely little pins?"

"They're called stock pins, Mom," Lisa said, sounding impatient. "You wear them on a stock—that's one of those collar things I wear in horse shows sometimes."

Mrs. Atwood shrugged. "Yes, all right, dear," she said, not even bothering to glance at Lisa. She was still staring expectantly at Tessa.

"We got them at the tack shop at the mall," Tessa said. "Veronica and I stopped by there because she wanted my advice about her wardrobe for the point-to-point."

"Oh, my!" Mrs. Atwood turned to stare worriedly at Lisa. "I hadn't even thought about that. I do hope you have something appropriate to wear, Lisa."

"Don't worry, Mom," Lisa said quickly. "I've got plenty of stuff to wear."

Carole stifled a laugh. She recognized the look of panic on Lisa's face. It appeared any time Mrs. Atwood seemed about to suggest a shopping trip. Mrs. Atwood loved to shop—especially when she could make Lisa try on lots of outfits while she was at it.

"Really," Lisa went on when Mrs. Atwood hesitated. "You just bought me those nice buff breeches, remember? I haven't even had a chance to wear them yet. And you said they'd look great with my good navy jacket, right?"

"Oh." Mrs. Atwood looked disappointed. "That's right." She glanced at Tessa again and brightened. "But

I've got a wonderful idea. Why don't we go and buy you one of those—er—stock pins, are they called? Then you can match Tessa and Veronica. Won't that be fun? We can go to the mall tomorrow afternoon." She smiled at the other girls. "You're all welcome to come along, of course."

"Sorry," Stevie said, not looking sorry at all. "I've got a doctor's appointment."

Carole felt guilty for abandoning Lisa, but she shook her head. "I can't make it, either. My dad has the day off tomorrow. I promised I'd go to the movies with him."

"Oh well," Mrs. Atwood said. "That's too bad. Tessa? How about you?"

"I'd love to," Tessa agreed.

Lisa looked relieved, which made Carole feel better. At least Lisa wouldn't be stuck shopping alone with her mother. "Okay, then," Carole said, waving a hand at the posters and lists and other materials spread over the floor. "Maybe we should get back to work. We can probably finish this stuff before dinner." *And maybe at the same time, we can convince Tessa she's making a big mistake by trusting Veronica,* she thought.

"Oh, that can wait." Mrs. Atwood leaned back against the cushions of the couch. "You girls are staying over, right? You'll have all night to work on these things." She smiled. "Now, Tessa, I want to hear all about your afternoon with Veronica. Don't leave out a thing."

"OH, TESSA, THERE you are!" Veronica rushed up to Carole and Tessa as they entered Pine Hollow's student locker room the next morning. "I thought you'd never get here."

Carole rolled her eyes. She wasn't in the mood for Veronica's games—whatever they were. She and Tessa had promised Max they would disinfect the manure pit. While most of the manure was spread in a nearby field to dry and then carted away to be used as fertilizer, a certain amount of the stuff just had to be dumped in the manure pit because there was only so much space in the field. The pit had to be cleaned out regularly, but this was one of the least popular tasks at Pine Hollow, which was the main reason that Carole had decided to volunteer when she and Tessa had overheard Max and Red O'Malley, the head stable hand, talking about it in the tack room. Carole knew that if The Saddle Club wanted to regain Max's respect, they would have to earn it.

"Hi, Veronica," Tessa greeted the other girl with a smile. "I wanted to thank you again for a lovely afternoon yesterday."

Veronica smiled back, looking pleased. "It was my pleasure," she purred. "But listen. I was thinking about what you said at the mall about those lemon yellow breeches you have back home. I've never had any that color, and I think they might look really good with my new tweed hacking jacket. But then I thought maybe my brown breeches were better. Will you come and look at the jacket with me and see what you think? Oh, and I found that spare ratcatcher shirt I was telling you about."

"Oh, brilliant!" Tessa exclaimed. "I can't imagine how I left mine at home. I was afraid I'd have to wear a T-shirt on Saturday."

"Don't worry about that," Veronica said. "My shirt will look great as part of your judging outfit—especially with your new stock pin. I thought you should try it on now so you'll know if it fits. If it doesn't, I'll have my tailor fix it. It's in my cubby. Come on, we can do it right now."

"Do you mind?" Tessa turned to Carole with an eager smile. "I know I promised to help you with the muck heap, but . . ."

Carole's heart sank. "Um, no, that's okay," she said

28

quietly. "Go ahead. I can take care of it myself. It's no big deal."

CAROLE'S SHOULDERS WERE aching by the time she finished her task. Cleaning up the muck heap wasn't easy at the best of times, but doing it all by herself was even worse. A truck had arrived an hour before to pick up most of the actual manure, but Carole had to scrape up the remains, rinse the cement floor with water, then disinfect it. Several times she thought about seeking out Stevie and Lisa to help her, but she resisted the urge. She knew that Stevie was hurrying to get her own work finished before she had to leave for her checkup. And Lisa was planning to spend some extra time with Derby. Carole didn't want to interrupt that, since Lisa had only been riding the gelding for a short time. Besides, Carole thought as she scraped the cement with a heavy shovel, why should her friends suffer? This was all Veronica's fault.

And Tessa's, added a little voice inside her head. Carole shoved the thought aside. She had work to do.

When she was finally finished, Carole washed her hands in the tack room sink, then dragged herself down the aisle in search of her friends. She saw Belle in her stall, munching peacefully on a fresh flake of hay. Derby was alone, too, though his shining coat and perfectly combed mane attested to the fact that Lisa had been there recently. Carole stopped by Starlight's stall long enough to give him a pat and a few carrot pieces, then headed outside.

She found Stevie and Lisa by the outdoor ring. They were sitting on the fence, watching Mrs. Pennington drive Hodge and Podge around the ring. This time, instead of Max's battered old pony cart, the big horses were pulling a cart that Carole had never seen before.

"Wow," Carole remarked, forgetting about her sore muscles for a moment. "No wonder Mrs. Pennington was so eager to get her carriage down here. It's incredible!"

The vehicle had four spoked wheels, but that was the only thing it had in common with the pony cart. Mrs. Pennington was perched on a high bench seat of gleaming leather set just behind the smaller forward wheels. Between the large rear wheels was a second leather seat. A ribbed leather hood rose over the front seat, shading the driver from the late-morning sun. The hood, seats, and tires were black, while the body and spokes of the cart were a bright, glossy yellow.

Lisa nodded without taking her eyes off the horse-drawn vehicle. "She told us it's called a Spider Phaeton," she said. "A phaeton is a kind of four-wheeled cart from the late seventeen hundreds."

"Cool." Carole climbed onto the fence beside her friends, letting out an involuntary groan as her over-worked muscles protested.

Stevie turned to glance at her. "What's wrong?" she said. "And by the way, where's Tessa?"

30

Carole explained quickly. When she finished, Lisa's eyes were wide.

"You mean you cleaned up the muck heap all by yourself?" she said. "Why didn't you come get us to help you?"

"Or better yet, why didn't you get Red to help you?" Stevie added with a grin. She hated disinfecting the manure pit.

Carole shrugged. "I didn't want to drag you guys away from what you were doing. And I didn't want Max to think I was wimping out or something, so I didn't want him to hear I asked Red for help."

"Hi there," said a new voice from behind them. It was Miles Pennington.

"Hi," Lisa greeted him. "Your grandma looks great out there."

Miles smiled. "I know," he said, watching the team in the ring. "She's happy as a clam now that her rigs are finally here."

"Does she have more than one of those carts?" Carole asked, casting another admiring glance at the beautiful yellow-and-black vehicle.

"Not just like that one." Miles waved a hand at the phaeton. "That's her favorite. It's the one she uses the most. But she has half a dozen vehicles altogether—a curricle, a governess cart, a buckboard . . ."

"Hold on a second," Stevie said. "What in the world *are* all those things?"

31

Miles laughed good-naturedly. "Sorry. I guess I'm so used to Grandmother's obsession that I forget not everyone spends half their time talking about these things."

Carole smiled at him. This was probably the longest conversation The Saddle Club had had with Miles Pennington so far, and Carole was starting to think that the teenager might be a lot more interesting than she had suspected. At first he had seemed kind of formal and boring, without much to say. Now Carole wondered if she had simply mistaken good manners for dullness. Had she and her friends jumped to conclusions about Miles because they knew he was from a very wealthy, hoity-toity background? That wasn't really fair, Carole realized. Some rich people—like Veronica—might indeed be totally boring, annoying, and self-absorbed, but certainly there were plenty of others who were smart and interesting and friendly. Just look at Tessa. Her family was wealthy, and she was as different from Veronica as could be.

At least we thought she was, that little voice whispered to Carole before she could stop it. An image of Veronica and Tessa browsing together through the fanciest stores at the mall popped into her head.

She shook it off. Miles was still talking, and she wanted to hear what he had to say. Carole was always interested in learning new things about horses. Besides, she was being ridiculous. Tessa was only being polite to Veronica to avoid trouble—that was all.

Miles was explaining the differences among the various types of horse-drawn vehicles. "A phaeton was meant to be driven by its owner rather than a hired driver," he said, pointing to the cart in the ring. "They're light vehicles with four wheels. Aside from that, they come in all shapes and sizes. Have you ever heard the phrase 'surrey with the fringe on top'?"

Carole nodded. "That's a line in one of those old songs my dad's always singing while he washes the dishes," she said.

"Well, now you can tell him that a surrey is just one type of phaeton," Miles said with a chuckle. "As for Grandmother's other vehicles, the curricle is a two-wheeler—the only two-wheeled cart, as far as I know, that's pulled by a pair of horses rather than just one. Then there's the governess cart. That's a type of dogcart—"

"Dogcart?" Stevie grinned. "Is that a cart pulled by a bunch of beagles?"

All four of them laughed. "Nothing like that," Miles assured her. "Dogcarts are another kind of vehicle, with even more variations than phaetons. They got their name because they allowed enough space under the seats for the driver's hunting dogs. A governess cart is a variation on the theme. Instead of dogs, it's built to accommodate children, with high sides to keep them from falling out during a drive."

"Wow," Lisa said. "You know a lot about this stuff."

Miles shrugged. "I don't have much choice," he said cheerfully. "I suppose if I'd been old enough when Grandmother was younger, I'd know just as much about show jumping. She used to be quite good at that, too."

"We heard." Carole gazed for a moment at the elderly woman sitting ramrod-straight on the narrow seat of the phaeton. Mrs. Pennington was the picture of elegance as she expertly guided the two large, glossy-coated Cleveland Bays with the help of two pairs of long reins and a long-handled driving whip.

Carole couldn't help wondering if driving horses could really be a substitute for riding them. Still, she knew that if she couldn't ride for some reason, she would want to find another way to be around horses. It sounded as though Mrs. Pennington had felt exactly the same way— and found a creative solution.

"Oh, and I almost forgot," Miles added. "We also have a couple of sleighs for driving in the snow." He laughed. "I think that was one of the things that worried Grandmother the most about moving to Virginia. She was afraid we'd never get to use the sleighs because the weather is so much warmer here than back in Pennsylvania."

"We do get snow down here once in a while," Stevie said, swinging her legs against the fence. "But put it this way—it's probably a good thing that most of her carts have wheels and not runners."

Miles chuckled. "Maybe that's why Grandmother decided to buy a large road coach just before we moved. I think that means she's getting ready to try a four-in-hand."

"I know what that is," Carole said. "Two pairs of horses, one in front of the other."

"I guess that means she'll hitch both her teams together, right?" Lisa guessed. "Didn't you say she has another pair arriving soon?"

"That's right," Miles said. "But I don't think she's planning to harness them with Hodge and Podge. They wouldn't match very well." He winked conspiratorially. "Actually, I think it's just her excuse to buy more horses. She started talking about it as soon as she realized how much larger our new stable is than the old one."

"A woman after my own heart," Carole declared.

A few minutes later the girls said good-bye to Miles and went inside to look for Tessa.

"She probably needs rescuing by now," Stevie said. "Especially if Veronica has been boring her with fashion tips and stories about the lifestyles of the rich and ridiculous."

Carole nodded, but she wasn't so sure. Tessa hadn't seemed particularly reluctant to go along with Veronica. But she decided not to mention that to her friends. "They were going to try on some clothes," she said. "They must be in either the locker room or the bathroom."

"Let's check the locker room first," Lisa suggested.

When they arrived, the student locker room was completely empty. There were no riding lessons scheduled for that day, so many of the young riders who didn't own their own horses probably wouldn't even come to the stable. But the room showed evidence that at least a few people had used it recently. A pair of thick socks was drying on one of the long benches that stretched across the room in front of the student cubbyholes. A few other articles of clothing were draped here and there. An empty soda can sat atop the five-foot wall of cubbies.

"They're not here," Carole said. "Let's try the bathroom."

"Wait." Stevie was staring at something under one of the benches. She pointed. "Aren't those the brand-new custom-made boots Veronica was bragging about the other day?"

Carole shrugged. Veronica was always bragging about one piece of expensive clothing or another. Carole didn't pay much attention anymore.

But Lisa nodded. "Those are the ones," she confirmed. "They're real steeplechase boots. She ordered them as soon as she heard about the point-to-point."

Carole rolled her eyes. "Leave it to Veronica to spend tons of money on something she'll probably only wear a few times."

Stevie was still staring in the direction of the boots. She had a very strange expression on her face. "Check it out," she said in a too-casual voice. "Someone left a sandwich sitting there on the bench right above Veronica's boots."

Lisa glanced at her, then at the sandwich, then back again. "Uh-oh," she said. "Look, Stevie. You know we can't risk—"

Carole was thinking the same thing. She knew all too well how Stevie's mind worked. "Wait, Stevie. If Max catches you—"

But Stevie wasn't listening to either of her friends. She leaped forward and grabbed the sandwich. "Peanut butter and jelly," she said. "Perfect!"

Carole gulped. The sandwich looked positively disgusting. Someone had taken a couple of bites before abandoning it. Grape jelly and half-melted peanut butter were oozing out the sides. "Gross," she said. "That thing belongs in the trash."

"It looks like it was already in the trash," Lisa muttered. "Look, there's some dirt and stuff stuck in the peanut butter . . ."

Stevie still wasn't listening to her friends. Her eyes were gleaming. "You know, it wouldn't take much for this sandwich to fall off the bench." She sat down just above Veronica's new boots. "And if those boots just happen to be sitting here when that happens . . ."

Carole opened her mouth to protest as Stevie leaned forward, sandwich in hand and a wicked grin on her face. After that, things happened fast.

"All right, what's the big emergency?" a loud voice said, startling all three girls.

They whirled to face the door—just in time to see Max walk in, followed by Veronica and Tessa. And Max was staring straight at Stevie.

Lisa felt frozen in place. She tried to open her mouth to say something to distract Max, but her vocal chords wouldn't obey.

It was too late anyway. Max was glaring suspiciously at Stevie. "Stevie Lake," he barked. "What are you doing?"

Lisa gulped. Stevie couldn't have looked guiltier if she'd had a flashing neon sign on her forehead reading Prank in Progress. She was leaning forward with the gooey, dripping sandwich in one hand and the other hand stretched toward Veronica's boots.

As usual, Stevie reacted quickly. She smiled innocently at Max. Then she grabbed Veronica's boots and pushed them aside. "Don't worry, Max," she asked cheerfully. "I

39

was just moving these boots. I wouldn't want my sandwich to drip on them."

Lisa gulped and glanced at Max. Would he really fall for that story?

It didn't look like it. Max folded his arms across his chest and glowered suspiciously. Veronica smirked. Tessa looked confused.

Then Stevie did the only thing she could do. Lisa knew she couldn't have done it herself. She doubted Carole could have, either. In fact, she strongly suspected that Stevie Lake was the only person in the world who would actually have been able to raise that awful-looking sandwich to her mouth and take a big bite.

"Mmm," Stevie said, chewing and swallowing quickly. "That hits the spot. Mucking out Belle's stall and doing all those other stable chores really wakes up the old appetite."

Max was still frowning, but he shrugged. Then he turned to face Veronica. "Okay, Veronica," he said. "What did you drag me in here for? I was in the middle of something."

Veronica glared at Stevie. "Actually, Max . . . ," she began loudly.

Lisa opened her mouth again to interrupt before Veronica could say anything incriminating. She doubted that Veronica would admit to picking that sandwich out of the trash and planting it temptingly on the bench for Stevie to find—though Lisa was sure that was exactly what had happened. Still, if Max knew that those were Veronica's boots by Stevie's feet, his suspicions might be raised once again. Especially if Veronica made him take a good, close look at the flecks of trash and dirty fingerprints on the sandwich.

"Max!" she shouted suddenly. "I have to ask you something!"

Max turned to stare at her in surprise. Lisa felt her cheeks flush as she struggled to figure out what to say next.

Carole came to her rescue. "Um, Max," she said. "What Lisa was about to say is, we were just watching Mrs. Pennington driving her phaeton outside."

"That's very interesting," Veronica said sarcastically. "Now, as I was saying—"

Lisa didn't let her finish. "That's right, Max," she added hurriedly, shooting Carole a grateful look. "Miles was telling us more about driving, and it was really interesting. We were wondering if you were planning to take Mrs. Pennington up on her offer to come talk to us again sometime after her equipment arrived."

"Right," Carole added cheerfully. "Because now it's here!"

Max nodded thoughtfully. "That's right, she did offer to speak to Horse Wise again." Horse Wise was the name of Pine Hollow's branch of the United States Pony Club. It met every Saturday morning, and Max often invited speakers to teach the group about different aspects of horses and horse care. Mrs. Pennington had spoken about driving the week before.

"Whatever," Veronica broke in. "So anyway, Max, I wanted to tell you—"

"When do you think she could come?" Stevie interrupted, catching on to what her friends were doing. She surreptitiously set the remains of the sandwich on the bench and shoved it out of sight behind her.

Max didn't notice. "Well, the sooner the better, I suppose," he said, stroking his chin thoughtfully. "It would certainly be more convenient for her to do it before her stable is finished and Hodge and Podge move out of Pine Hollow. Obviously Saturday is out because of the point-to-point, though." The Horse Wise meeting was canceled because most of the members would be riding in or at least attending the point-to-point.

"How about tomorrow's lessons?" Carole spoke up.

Max looked surprised. "Tomorrow?" he said slowly. "Well, that's not much notice. But it would be nice to give you a little bit of a break from all the jumping we've been doing lately. Besides—"

"The sooner the better, right?" Lisa finished for him. She glanced at her watch. "Uh-oh. The Penningtons were just finishing up when we left them a little while ago. If you want to catch them before they leave—"

Max nodded briskly. "Right," he agreed. "I'd better go now." With that, he hurried out of the room.

When he was gone, Veronica gave Stevie, Carole, and

Lisa a sour look. "You three are just full of clever ideas, aren't you?" she said cryptically. Then she turned to smile at Tessa. "Listen, Tessa," she said in a friendlier voice. "I was just thinking. I'd really like for you to see the rest of my riding clothes. Maybe you could find more stuff to borrow. Do you want to come over this afternoon after we're finished here? We could have tea again. I asked the maid to make some real English-style scones."

"Smashing," Tessa began agreeably. "That sounds like—" Then she glanced at Lisa and stopped herself. "Oh, but I can't this afternoon," she corrected. "Lisa's mum is taking us to the mall. Perhaps another time."

"Sure." Veronica gave Lisa an irritated glance. Then she smiled at Tessa and shrugged. "Far be it from me to stand in the way of shopping." She said good-bye to Tessa, mumbled something relatively polite to the rest of The Saddle Club, then left.

"Wow," Stevie said when she was gone. "That was close."

"What was that all about?" Tessa asked. She set down the silky white shirt she was holding and sat beside Stevie. "Veronica and I were chatting in the tack room, and suddenly she insisted on rushing in here with Max in tow."

"Oh, nothing much." Carole rolled her eyes. "Just another one of Veronica's nasty little tricks." She told Tessa the whole story.

43

At the end, Tessa looked unconvinced. "Are you sure she set it up?" she said skeptically. "It sounds a bit far-fetched."

"Not for Veronica." Stevie wiped a glob of peanut butter off her fingers onto her jeans. "She'll do anything to make us look bad. Especially now, when she knows Max is on our case."

"Oh, well," Tessa said with a shrug. "In any case, no harm done." She winked and grinned. "Perhaps one of us will come up with a sneaky way to get back at her some-time soon."

Carole looked surprised. "I thought you wanted to keep things friendly," she said. "I thought that's why you've been putting up with her boring conversation for the past two days."

"Well, I do want to keep things calm," Tessa admitted. "Besides, she's really not as dull as you all seem to think. I've found some of the things she says very, very interest-ing."

Lisa shrugged. She didn't feel like arguing about it right then—especially since it was almost time for her mother to pick them up for their trip to the mall.

She grabbed the peanut butter sandwich from behind Stevie and tossed it into the trash can with a shudder. "Well, I just have one more thing to say about all this," she told Stevie.

"What's that?" Stevie asked.

Lisa grinned weakly. "After watching you eat that horrible sandwich, I think it's a good thing you're going to the doctor today anyway."

"OH, LOOK AT this lovely silk shirt, dear!" Mrs. Atwood exclaimed, holding up a bright turquoise-and-magenta-checked blouse for Lisa's inspection. "Isn't it stylish? And it looks just like those outfits professional jockeys wear. Wouldn't it be fun for you to wear it in your race on Saturday?"

Lisa sighed. It was a couple of hours later. Mrs. Atwood had arrived right on schedule to pick up Lisa and Tessa, and ever since they had arrived at the mall she had been doing her usual thing—namely, trying to interest Lisa in all sorts of clothes and accessories she didn't want or need.

"I'm not certain, Mrs. Atwood," Tessa said politely, "but that may not be appropriate for this sort of event. I think most of the riders will be dressed in traditional hunting-style clothing rather than jockey's silks."

Lisa shot her a grateful look. She had Tessa to thank for the fact that she was only *half* miserable rather than completely miserable. Tessa had managed to distract Mrs. Atwood just enough to keep her from driving Lisa totally crazy. Lisa knew that her mother was terribly impressed by Tessa's title, her manners, and her upper-class British accent. Because of all that, Mrs. Atwood was actually paying much more attention to Tessa than she was to Lisa, and for that Lisa was thankful.

Mrs. Atwood reluctantly hung the silk blouse back on its rack. "Well, if you say so, dear," she told Tessa. "You're much more of an expert on these matters than I am, of course." She headed for the next rack. "Oh, but what about these wonderful tweed jackets . . . ," she began eagerly.

"Well, hello!" a familiar voice called cheerfully. "Fancy meeting you here!"

"Veronica?" Lisa muttered. She turned, and sure enough, Veronica was hurrying toward them across the wide center aisle of the department store.

"Hello, Veronica," Mrs. Atwood said. "What a pleasant surprise! Are you doing some shopping for the point-to-point? Your mother tells me you're entered in the junior hurdle race."

"That's right," Veronica said pleasantly. "Actually, I was just trying to figure out what I should wear." She sighed. "Unfortunately, I'm having some trouble. That's why I was so excited when I saw Tessa over here. She knows so much about riding clothes."

Tessa looked a little surprised. Lisa thought she knew why. Tessa actually did know quite a bit about riding attire—all the girls did—but unlike Veronica, she wasn't really very interested in the subject. As long as her clothes were comfortable and safe for riding, she was content.

But Mrs. Atwood was nodding agreeably. "Oh, yes,"

she told Veronica. "Dear Tessa has been such a help to us today."

"I'm sure she has," Veronica said smoothly. Then she smiled beseechingly at Tessa and Mrs. Atwood, completely ignoring Lisa. "It's such a nice coincidence that I ran into you. I wonder if I could steal Tessa away for a little while? There's a pair of breeches in another store that I'd just love to show her."

"Certainly," Mrs. Atwood said. She patted Tessa on the arm. "Lisa and I can make do by ourselves if you'd like to run along and help Veronica. We could meet you by the entrance when it's time to go."

"Oh, don't worry about that," Veronica said quickly. "I can drop Tessa off at your house when we're finished. Is that okay?"

"It's fine with me," Mrs. Atwood said. "Tessa?"

Tessa hesitated, glancing at Lisa. Lisa forced herself to keep her expression neutral, since her mother was looking at her. If Mrs. Atwood knew that she absolutely hated the thought of Tessa and Veronica spending any more time together, Lisa would never hear the end of it. Besides, Lisa was sure Tessa would manage to back out of Veronica's invitation gracefully all on her own.

But to her surprise, Tessa's face broke into an eager grin. "Sure, I'd love to," she said. She stepped forward and slipped her hand cozily into the crook of Veronica's arm. "Lead the way."

Veronica smiled with satisfaction. "Great," she said. "Let's go."

Tessa glanced back over her shoulder and winked at Lisa as she hurried off with Veronica. "See you at home," she called.

Lisa didn't bother to reply. Her shoulders slumped as she realized that her mother was already gathering a whole new set of clothes to show her.

She was doomed.

"DID YOU ACTUALLY end up buying anything after all that?" Carole asked.

Lisa sighed and leaned back against the wall of the upstairs hallway. She was on the phone with Carole and Stevie. Stevie's family had three-way calling, which came in handy for telephone Saddle Club meetings like this one. "Not much," she said. "Just a few new pairs of socks and a shirt. At least I talked her out of that stock pin. You wouldn't believe how much it cost."

"What I can't believe is that Tessa isn't back yet," Stevie said. "What time did you say she went off with Veronica?"

"Hours ago," Lisa replied.

"Poor Tessa." Carole sounded sympathetic. "She must be bored stiff."

Lisa sighed again and played with the buttons on her shirt. "To be honest, I'm not feeling all that sorry for her right now," she admitted. "I mean, it wasn't as though Veronica dragged her off kicking and screaming. She didn't even have to beg very hard. Tessa practically jumped at the chance to go off with her."

"Are you sure she wasn't just sick of your mom?" Stevie asked. "Uh, no offense or anything."

"None taken," Lisa said. "And I thought of that. Mom was being her usual self, more or less. But still, I wouldn't have expected Tessa to abandon me. She knew I was counting on her to help me survive the shopping marathon."

"Good point," Carole said. "It was practically her duty as a member of The Saddle Club to stay with you. Besides, getting away from your mom to shop with Veronica would just be jumping out of the frying pan into the fire."

"A roaring bonfire," Stevie agreed wholeheartedly. She paused, and Lisa could almost hear the wheels turning in her head. "No, I think there must be something else going on here."

"What do you mean?" Carole asked.

"I mean I think something is going on with Tessa," Stevie said. "Or Veronica. Or maybe both."

"That clears things up," Lisa said dryly. She switched the phone to her other ear. "But I was thinking about it, and I was wondering if we're just missing what's staring us in the face here."

"What's that?" Carole asked.

Lisa bit her lip. She could hardly bring herself to say the words out loud. "Maybe," she said, "just maybe, Tessa and Veronica actually . . . like each other."

Carole gasped. "No way," she said quickly. "Tessa is a member of The Saddle Club. And Veronica is, well . . ."

"Pure evil?" Stevie suggested helpfully.

Carole laughed wryly. "Well, I was going to say Veronica is Veronica," she said. "But either way you look at it, it just doesn't make sense."

"I guess not," Lisa said. But she didn't feel very confident about her own words. "Still, maybe it's nothing that extreme. We know Tessa was upset because she thought she was going to be responsible for us losing our riding privileges."

"But that's ridiculous," Stevie protested. "It would be Veronica's fault if that happened, not hers."

"Wait," Carole said. "I think I see what you're saying, Lisa. No matter what we'd say, Tessa would still feel guilty if Max kicked us out for fighting back when Veronica was being mean to her."

Lisa had to pause to run Carole's complicated sentence through her head. Then she nodded into the phone. "Right," she said. "Maybe this is just Tessa's way of calming the troubled waters. Or whatever."

"Maybe," Carole said eagerly. "That would make sense. Should we just come right out and ask her about it?"

Lisa hesitated. She couldn't help remembering how Tessa had acted at the mall. She hadn't seemed like someone who was reluctantly going along with something to keep the peace. In fact, she had seemed downright thrilled to rush off with Veronica. "I don't know," she said at last. "Maybe we should wait a few days and see what happens."

"Are you sure?" Stevie sounded worried. "Don't forget, last time we tried to keep a secret from Tessa—"

"I know." Lisa cut her off. When the girls had tried to hide their probation from Tessa, it had made them all miserable. "But this is different. We're not really hiding anything from her." She shrugged, though she knew her friends couldn't see her. "If anything, she's the one hiding something from us."

There was a long moment of silence as they all thought that over.

Suddenly Carole spoke up. "Oops," she said worriedly. "I hear Dad calling me. I just remembered I was supposed to set the table. I'd better go."

"Me too," Stevie said. "I just saw my brother Michael walk by with his aquarium of pet frogs. That can't be good news."

Lisa grinned briefly at that in spite of her worries about Tessa. "Okay," she said. "I'll keep you posted. We're all meeting before lessons tomorrow, right?"

"Right," Carole replied.

"Definitely," Stevie said at the same time. "And don't forget—Max said it was okay for Phil to come to lessons and watch the carriage demonstration." Thanks to The

51

Saddle Club's idea, Mrs. Pennington had agreed to bring over one of her fancy horse-drawn vehicles the next day and give another demonstration for the intermediate riding class. Stevie had decided to find out if her boyfriend could attend, since she knew he was always interested in any new horse-related topic.

"And we're all going to TD's for ice cream afterward, right?" Lisa said.

"Yep," Stevie confirmed. "It should be fun. And it will give Phil and Tessa a chance to get to know each other better. They only met that one time last week."

After that the three girls said good-bye and hung up. Lisa returned the phone to its spot on the table, then wandered downstairs.

"Are you finished with the phone, Lisa?" Mrs. Atwood called from the kitchen. "I need to make a few calls."

"I'm finished, Mom." Lisa was relieved. As long as her mother was on the phone, she couldn't put Lisa to work on more projects for the point-to-point.

Lisa wasn't sure she could concentrate on equipment lists or menus or sponsor addresses right then. She was too worried about Tessa. The incident at the mall had disturbed her more than she'd been willing to admit to the others. It wasn't just that Tessa had gone with Veronica. That was bad enough. But why had she seemed so excited about it? Could her earlier, horrible theory be right? Could Tessa actually *like* spending time with the snobby girl? Could she—Could she possibly like Veronica *better* than she liked The Saddle Club?

Lisa's head had been throbbing with these thoughts since she'd gotten home from the mall. Putting a hand to her forehead, she decided she had to distract herself somehow. She was on her way into the living room to see what was on TV when the front door flew open and Tessa hurried in, smiling and breathless. "Oh, hi, Lisa!" she said, waving a bulging shopping bag. "I finally made it home!"

"Hi," Lisa said dully.

Tessa didn't seem to notice Lisa's gloomy tone. "Whew, I have *got* to sit down right now," she declared with a laugh. "My feet are killing me!"

Lisa didn't answer. She just followed Tessa into the living room, amazed at her cheerful mood. If Lisa had just spent several hours shopping with Veronica diAngelo, she'd have been ready to strangle someone by now. So would Stevie and Carole—Phil, too, for that matter, along with just about every other out-of-town member of The Saddle Club. But not Tessa. She looked as happy as ever.

Tessa flopped down on the living room couch, still clutching her shopping bag. "I'm exhausted!" she declared happily. "We must have walked ten kilometers today going up and down that mall."

"I can imagine," Lisa said dryly. "Shopping with Veronica must be a tiring experience. Buying things is probably her greatest talent. I'm surprised you only came back with one bag."

Her sarcasm was lost on Tessa, who sat up and smiled. "That reminds me," she said. "I got you something." She reached into her shopping bag and pulled out a small rose-colored box.

Lisa was surprised. She took the box and stared at it blankly. "What is it?" she asked.

Tessa giggled. "Open it, silly," she urged. "That's the best way to find out, isn't it?"

Lisa lifted the lid of the box. Inside, nestled on a bed of cotton, was a slender silver pin. She gasped. "A stock pin!"

Tessa nodded. "I could tell you weren't mad about those gold ones Veronica and I got yesterday," she said frankly. "But when I saw this one, I thought it might be more your style."

"It is." Lisa picked up the pin to take a better look. Suddenly her irritation melted away, and she felt guilty about her earlier doubts. What had she and her friends been thinking? Just because Tessa was polite enough to put up with Veronica, that didn't mean they should start concocting all sorts of ridiculous theories about it. "It's just my style. Thanks, Tessa. I love it!"

At that moment Mrs. Atwood hurried into the room. "Oh, hello, Tessa," she said. "I thought I heard you come in. Did you have a nice time with Veronica?"

"Oh, yes," Tessa said. "She's such an interesting person. She has a marvelously witty way of looking at the world."

"Her mother is just the same way," Mrs. Atwood assured Tessa, sitting down beside her on the couch. "She's done a wonderful job of raising Veronica to know her own mind. Such a smart and well-spoken young girl!"

"Absolutely," Tessa agreed. "Just now in the limo, Veronica told me the most interesting story about her last trip to Paris. . . ."

Lisa gritted her teeth as her mother and Tessa continued to praise the diAngelos. She studied the gorgeous silver stock pin in her hand. It had been such a thoughtful, personal gift, and she knew Stevie and Carole would agree. Only a good friend could have chosen it—a friend like Tessa.

So why did it sometimes seem that none of them really knew Tessa at all?

STEVIE CHECKED HER watch for the fifth time in thirty seconds. It was almost time for riding lessons to start, and the four members of The Saddle Club were already seated on the fence of the outdoor ring. Because of the carriage-driving demonstration, Max had told everyone not to bother tacking up their horses, so most of the class was already outside, talking or just enjoying the bright summer day.

Tessa laughed. "Really, Stevie," she teased. "If you don't stop looking at that wristwatch every other second, you'll wear it out!"

Carole noticed what Stevie was doing, too. "Don't worry," she said with a smile. "I'm sure Phil will be here soon."

Stevie grinned sheepishly. She knew her friends were probably right. Phil would get there when he got there, and unless she missed her guess, he would make sure to be there in plenty of time for the demonstration. But she couldn't help glancing at her watch again a few seconds later.

Phil lived in a town about ten miles away and rode at a different stable, so he and Stevie only got to see each other once or twice a month. During the summer it was usually easier to get together, but Stevie still appreciated every visit. Besides, she really did want him to spend some time with Tessa before she had to go back to England.

Stevie was checking her watch yet again when she heard a car turn up the driveway. "There he is," she said with relief, recognizing the Marstens' car.

Moments later, Phil was perched on the fence between Stevie and Tessa. "I'm glad I made it in time," he said breathlessly. "My sister Barbara promised to drop me off on her way to the mall, and she kept changing her mind about which earrings she was going to wear." Barbara was Phil's oldest sister.

"Never mind," Tessa said cheerily. "You're here now, and that's what matters. By the way, Stevie was telling me the other night about the riding camp where you two met. Did she really single-handedly save all the horses at camp from a huge barn fire?"

Phil rolled his eyes and laughed. "Leave it to Stevie to

exaggerate, as usual," he said teasingly. "Listen, this is what *really* happened. . . ."

Stevie smiled as Tessa and Phil continued to chat. She was glad they seemed to like each other as much as she liked both of them.

Then her attention was drawn by a flurry of activity in the ring. Red had just entered, pushing one of Pine Hollow's wheelbarrows. Instead of being loaded with manure or hay bales or any other familiar stable items, it was full of bright orange rubber cones.

Carole was watching Red, too, a puzzled look on her face. "What's he doing with those?" she asked. "They look like traffic cones."

Several other students had noticed the cones, too. "Yo, Red," Joe Novick called out. "What's up with the cones? Are you practicing to get your driver's license?"

Red smiled good-naturedly as several kids laughed. "You'll have to wait and see," he called back. "I've been sworn to secrecy."

As The Saddle Club and their classmates watched, Red dragged the wheelbarrow to the center of the ring. He dug under the stack of cones for a moment, finally coming up with a measuring tape. He grabbed one cone, dropped it on the dusty ground, then carefully measured out a distance of several yards starting from the edge of the cone.

"What in the world is he doing?" Lisa said.

Stevie shrugged, but she noticed that Carole didn't

look quite as confused as the rest of them did. "Do you know something we don't know?" Stevie asked her.

"I'm not sure," Carole said. "This looks sort of familiar. I think I may have seen something like this at a horse show once."

"Something like what?" Phil asked.

Carole shook her head. "Just wait," she said. "If it's what I think it is, you'll find out soon."

Stevie wasn't about to let her friend get away with that. But before she could ask any more questions, she heard a loud snort from the stable entrance behind her. She turned and saw Hodge and Podge emerging with Miles at their heads. The Cleveland Bays were groomed to within an inch of their lives. They were outfitted in a perfectly polished silver-jointed leather harness and pulling the yellow-and-black phaeton.

"Wow," Lisa said. "They look amazing."

Everyone else seemed to agree. All the riding students watched as Miles led the horses into the ring, keeping them at one end so that he wouldn't get in Red's way.

A moment later Max and Mrs. Pennington came out of the stable and walked to the ring. Max was wearing his normal riding clothes. Mrs. Pennington, however, looked just as fancy as her horses did. She was wearing an old-fashioned long skirt and jacket, and an elaborate feathered hat was perched atop her iron-gray curls. Curvy-heeled buckled shoes and long, buttoned gloves completed the outfit.

"Attention, everyone," Max said, walking to the center of the ring. "I think you all know Mrs. Pennington, who spoke at our last Horse Wise meeting. She has graciously agreed to give us another driving demonstration now that her equipment is here."

Stevie was only half listening as Max went on to say a few more words about Mrs. Pennington and her accomplishments. She was busy watching Red. The stable hand had just finished distributing the cones, and now he pulled the wheelbarrow out of the ring. But Stevie could see that there was still one item left inside—a paper grocery bag. As she watched, Red picked up the bag, tucked it under his arm, and quietly reentered the ring. He walked to the nearest cone, then dipped his hand into the bag.

Stevie leaned forward for a better look. She was more confused than ever when Red pulled out an ordinary yellow tennis ball and set it carefully on the narrow top of the cone. The ball settled comfortably into the small opening there. Red moved on to the next cone, and the one after that. By the time Max had finished his introductory speech, every one of the orange cones had a bright yellow ball perched on it.

"All right, then," Max said at last. "Mrs. Pennington, if you're ready to start . . ."

The elderly woman nodded and stepped forward to address the class. "First of all," she said in her clear, confident voice, "I want to give you a little demonstration. Some of you may be under the impression that there is

only one way to have an exciting time with a horse—
namely, by sitting on his back. I want to show you that
driving can be just as much fun."

She walked toward the phaeton and held out her hand.
Max stepped up gallantly and offered his arm, helping her
up the high step into the old-fashioned vehicle.

Soon Mrs. Pennington was sitting on the front seat.
She took up the double reins in her left hand and the
long, thin whip in her right. Miles stepped away from the
team and headed for the fence to join the students. With
a flick of Mrs. Pennington's wrists, the big horses stepped
off in perfect harmony.

Stevie forgot about the mysterious cones for a moment
as she watched Hodge and Podge walk and trot around
the perimeter of the ring. Mrs. Pennington sat almost
perfectly still. Using only her hands, her voice, and a
long-handled whip, she kept her horses moving exactly
where she wanted them.

Finally she brought her team to a square halt at the far
end of the ring, just a few yards from one set of orange
cones. There was a smattering of applause from the students. Stevie felt like adding a few whoops and hollers of
appreciation—Hodge and Podge deserved it—but somehow, looking at the impeccably dressed older woman, she
decided that that wouldn't quite be dignified. She clapped
loudly instead.

Mrs. Pennington acknowledged the reaction with a re-
gal nod of her head. Then she turned to address Max.

"Mr. Regnery, the stopwatch, if you please," she called to him.

Max nodded and reached into his pocket. He pulled out the timer he sometimes used during class. "Ready when you are, Mrs. Pennington," he called back.

"All right, then," the woman said. She turned to face the students again. "Now I'm pleased to introduce you to a sport you may not have seen before. Back in Devon, Pennsylvania, we know it as scurry driving." She pointed to the cones scattered about the ring. "Please note that we have several pairs of orange cones. My goal is to drive my team through this course as quickly as possible without knocking over the cones or dislodging the balls on top of them."

"I knew it," Carole whispered gleefully to her friends. "I saw this kind of thing at a show a long time ago before I moved to Virginia. It's really fun—big, fancy carts like that one go racing around the course, and the fastest cart wins."

The others didn't have a chance to respond. Mrs. Pennington had started.

Stevie never would have believed that horses as large as Hodge and Podge could move so nimbly. They broke into a brisk trot as they headed straight between the first pair of cones, then sped up into a rolling canter. Stevie gasped as the Cleveland Bays whirled around a tight turn, then headed for the next pair of cones at a sharp angle. She almost closed her eyes, sure that Hodge's big hooves were going to smash right into the left-hand cone. But Mrs. Pennington flicked her whip just above Hodge's shoulder, and he adjusted his stride just enough to miss the cone. The phaeton slid between the two cones with mere inches to spare on each side.

Stevie watched with growing admiration as Mrs. Pennington guided her team through the rest of the brief course. She was amazed that the driver could judge so accurately the exact moment she had to ask the horses to turn or slow down. But the team raced between each pair of cones without so much as brushing them with a hoof or one of the phaeton's big wooden wheels, even though the horses kept up a brisk speed throughout, moving smoothly from trot to canter and back again. When Mrs. Pennington pulled Hodge and Podge to a stop with a flourish, every ball remained squarely in place.

This time everyone who was watching broke into loud applause, and Stevie wasn't the only one whooping and hollering. "That was amazing!" Phil shouted over the noise as Mrs. Pennington tipped her hat to her fans.

"Totally," Stevie agreed. "I guess she was right. Carriage driving isn't boring at all!"

When the applause died down, Max held up his stopwatch. "If you think that was exciting, listen to this," he called. "In a real scurry event at a horse show, there would be a dozen or so entries who would have to complete the course just as Mrs. Pennington and her team did. Each round would be timed, with faults taken for knocking down a ball or a cone or going over the time allowed. The fastest time with the fewest faults would win."

"Just like show jumping," Lisa commented.

Max heard her and nodded. "It's the same basic idea," he said.

Mrs. Pennington drove her team closer to the students, then stopped. "It's a fun event," she said, sounding just slightly breathless, though she looked as calm and composed as ever. "One misjudged step can mean a smashed cone and a disastrous score. It's vital to be accurate." She smiled. "But if you want to win, you must be fast as well. And that's where the fun comes in—for the teams and for the audience." She waved a hand at her own outfit. "Of course, the audience also enjoys seeing the turnouts. At the Devon Horse Show in Pennsylvania, where I compete each year, the scurry driving event is limited to pairs pulling four-wheeled antique carriage vehicles. That can mean anything from a dashing little phaeton like this one"—she gestured to her own carriage—"to a massive antique police wagon or grocer's cart. And naturally, the drivers usually dress to match their vehicles."

Stevie sighed dreamily. "That sounds so cool," she said. "I'd love to see a real scurry contest like that." She couldn't believe she had never heard of scurry driving before. It was just the sort of thing she loved the most—a real athletic equine endeavor requiring skill and talent, but also requiring at least a little bit of wackiness.

"You'd love it," Carole assured her.

Suddenly Tessa grinned. She stood up on the lowest rail of the fence and waved her hand at Max. "Max!" she called excitedly. "I've just had a smashing idea!"

"What is it, Tessa?" Max asked.

"Why don't we see if we can add a scurry race to the point-to-point event on Saturday?" Tessa said.

There were cries of approval from all around. Stevie could tell that after Mrs. Pennington's exciting demonstration, many of the other students were just as eager as she was to see a full-scale race.

But she could also see that Max wasn't quite as enthusiastic about the idea. "I don't know, Tessa," he said. "That would be lots of fun, I'll admit. But at this late date—"

"Why not?" Polly Giacomin called out. "It would be a blast!" Several other people shouted out their agreement as Mrs. Pennington looked on with a bemused expression.

Max held up his hands for quiet. "Just a minute," he said firmly. "Now, I'm not saying that it wouldn't be a good addition to the day. I just think it might be better to suggest it if there's another point-to-point next year. It's just too late this year." He glanced over at Mrs. Pennington and smiled. "For one thing, as of right now, we would have only one entry."

"Make that two entries," Mrs. Pennington corrected, still looking bemused. "My second team is due to arrive before the weekend, and my grandson is quite an accomplished driver himself. I'm not saying he'd stand a chance

65

against me"—she gave the watching students a droll wink—"but it would be good practice for him."

Miles pretended to be insulted as the students laughed. "You'd better watch what you say, Grandmother!" he called out. "You'll be sorry when I don't let you touch my blue ribbon."

Max still looked unconvinced. "I'm sorry," he said. "I just don't think—"

"I know someone else who might want to enter," Polly interrupted. "One of my neighbors has a cousin who has a carriage team."

Phil raised his hand. "I could ask Mr. Baker if he wants to give it a shot," he called out. Mr. Baker was the head instructor at Cross County, the stable where Phil rode. "He's got a fancy old carriage he drives in parades once in a while."

"And some of us could enter with a couple of ponies and the pony cart," Carole spoke up. "That's got four wheels. Are ponies allowed to enter?"

"Certainly," Mrs. Pennington answered before Max could reply. "The only rule is that you must have a pair. There's no limit to how large or small the animals can be."

That reminded Stevie of something. "Mr. Toll!" she blurted out excitedly. "I mean, what about that farmer Mr. Toll who lives near here? He has a couple of teams of big workhorses, remember? He could enter with his hay wagon."

That did it. Suddenly everyone seemed to remember a

neighbor, a relative, or a friend of a friend with some connection to a carriage team. Before long Max threw up his hands in exasperation, but he was smiling. "All right, all right!" he shouted over the racket. "You win. I'll speak to the country club committee. If they agree, I'll offer to help organize a scurry race for the point-to-point."

The students let out a loud cheer. Miles Pennington joined in, and even Mrs. Pennington let out a hearty "Hear, hear!"

Max raised one finger warningly. "But remember, you all promised to help."

"We'll help, Max," Carole promised. "You can count on us."

"And on Miles and me, too," Mrs. Pennington added. "I'd be happy to help organize the event."

"Good." Max smiled at Mrs. Pennington. "Now, I believe our guest speaker has some more to tell us about driving."

LISA SLID DOWN off the fence as soon as Max dismissed the class half an hour later. "I'll meet you guys inside," she told her friends hurriedly. "I want to call my mom right away. You know—break it to her gently."

"Oh dear," Tessa said, looking worried. "I didn't even think about that when I suggested the scurry race. Do you suppose your mum will be terribly frantic?"

"Probably," Carole answered for Lisa. "But don't worry. That's the way she is. Right, Lisa?"

Lisa smiled weakly in response, then hurried inside, heading for the pay phone in the hallway outside the locker room. She wasn't sure whether to be happy or upset about the new addition to the point-to-point schedule. On the one hand, she could understand why her friends and classmates were so excited. Mrs. Pennington's scurry run had been fun to watch. On the other hand, she could only imagine how much more work this would mean for her mother—and therefore for The Saddle Club. It wasn't that Lisa had anything against hard work. It was just—well, she wasn't sure *what* was bothering her exactly. Perhaps she wished that Tessa had run the idea past her friends before blurting it out to the larger group. Not that Lisa would have voted against it, of course. It was just that . . . well . . .

Lisa was starting to confuse herself. She pushed her muddled thoughts aside and decided to concentrate on the best way to tell her mother. After all, it was done now, no matter what she thought of it. All she could do was deal with it.

Mrs. Atwood took the news better than Lisa would have expected. In fact, she hardly seemed fazed at all by the idea of adding another event to the day's schedule—especially when she heard that Mrs. Pennington was involved.

"Don't worry about a thing, dear," Mrs. Atwood trilled. "I'm sure we can manage to pull it all together somehow."

"Okay, Mom. Bye." Lisa shrugged as she hung up.

Sometimes people were hard to figure out, even when you thought you knew them.

Lisa wanted to visit Prancer and Derby, but first she set out in search of her friends. She thought she might suggest a sleepover at her house that evening. Despite her mother's calm response, Lisa was still sure that this turn of events would mean there was suddenly a lot more work to be done.

She found Carole, Stevie, and Phil still perched on the fence around the outdoor ring. Most of the other students had dispersed, and the Penningtons and their team were nowhere in sight. Only the phaeton remained, parked just outside the gate.

"What are you guys still doing out here?" Lisa asked as she approached. "And where's Tessa?"

"Take a guess." Stevie's voice was grumpy.

Phil rolled his eyes. "She just went off with Veronica," he told Lisa. "And these two won't explain why. They're being very mysterious."

"She went with Veronica?" Lisa's heart sank. "What do you mean?"

Carole shrugged. She looked almost as disgruntled as Stevie did. "Remember how Mrs. Pennington said she'd help out with the scurry race?" she said. "Well, Veronica rushed right over after class and volunteered herself and Tessa to help out. They're inside making plans with the Penningtons right now."

"I don't get it." Phil looked completely confused. "Why

would Veronica want Tessa to come with her? Isn't Tessa *your* friend? Last I heard, that would definitely make her *not* Veronica's friend."

Stevie sighed impatiently. "We'll explain it all later," she said. "Right now, we have to—"

Stevie bit back her words as Tessa and Veronica emerged from the stable and came hurrying toward the group. Both of them were smiling, looking flushed and excited.

"Super! You're still here," Tessa said. "You don't mind if I go over to the Penningtons' house with Veronica a little later, do you?"

Lisa shrugged and did her best not to frown. "Why would we mind?"

"Brilliant," Tessa declared happily. She glanced over her shoulder. "Come on, Veronica. We'd better get back inside."

"Right," Veronica agreed. She smirked at Stevie, Carole, and Lisa. "Mrs. Pennington asked the two of us *specifically* to take care of her gorgeous harnesses," she bragged.

Stevie raised one eyebrow skeptically. "You mean clean them?" she said. "Are you sure you know how?"

Veronica gave Stevie an irritated look. Then she turned to Phil. "Phil, could you come and help us?" she wheedled, smiling at him brightly. "We need some help carrying all that heavy harness to the tack room, and you're the strongest one around here."

Phil looked a little suspicious. Lisa didn't blame him

one bit. Usually Veronica acted just as obnoxious toward him as she did toward any other member of The Saddle Club. But he shrugged agreeably. "Sure," he said, sliding down from the fence.

"Great," Veronica said smugly. "While you're at it, maybe you can tell us a little more about that Cross County driving team you mentioned. That way we can fill in the Penningtons when we go over there later."

Phil shrugged again. "Okay." He cast an apologetic glance at the other girls. "I'll be back soon. Then we can head over to TD's."

Tessa gasped. "Oh no!" she cried. "I forgot all about that when I told Mrs. Pennington I could make it this afternoon." She bit her lip, looking anxious as she glanced from Veronica to the other girls and back.

Lisa waited for Tessa to make her excuses to Veronica. After all, the trip to TD's wasn't just an ice cream break. It was supposed to be a Saddle Club meeting. That was important.

But Tessa wasn't looking at Veronica now. She was looking at Lisa and the other girls. "Um," she began hesitantly.

Stevie didn't let her finish. "Don't worry about it," she said shortly. "We can all go to TD's another time."

"Right," Carole added. "It's no problem."

"Really?" Tessa looked relieved. "Thanks, guys." She turned to face Veronica and Phil, looking excited again. "Right then—let's go get that harness!"

The three of them hurried off. Lisa watched them go, feeling slightly queasy. "So, what do you think now?" she asked. "What's going on with Tessa and Veronica?"

Carole shook her head, looking grim. "I was really trying to look on the bright side," she said. "You know—that Tessa was just being nice."

"Missing a Saddle Club meeting to hang out and swap shopping stories with Veronica goes *way* beyond just being nice," Stevie snapped.

Lisa nodded sadly. "It's totally weird. Kind of like one of those nightmares you have sometimes that don't make any sense, but you still know they're scary."

Her friends nodded. "What do we do now?" Carole asked.

"What *can* we do?" Stevie shrugged. "Let's go check on our horses. Then we'll rescue Phil and head over to TD's. If anything calls for a Saddle Club meeting, it's this."

"READY?" STEVIE ASKED a short while later, poking her head into Starlight's stall.

"Just about." Carole didn't look up. She was busy trying to pry a small stone out of her horse's rear left foot with a hoof pick. Lisa was in the stall, too, standing near Starlight's head and talking to him soothingly.

"Having trouble?" Stevie asked, immediately taking in the problem. She could see that Starlight had managed to get the stone stuck deep in the point of his frog. "Want some help?"

72

"Thanks." Carole looked relieved as she handed over the hoof pick. "I just can't get under it."

Stevie nodded and got to work. She was known around Pine Hollow to be especially handy with a hoof pick. Within seconds, she had worked the tip of the pick beneath the stone and popped it out. "There," she said, lowering Starlight's hoof to the floor. "Good as new."

Starlight snorted and turned to roll his eyes at Stevie over his shoulder. He shifted his weight onto the foot she had just let go and tossed his head.

Stevie grinned and patted him on the hindquarters. "You're welcome, boy," she said. "Always happy to help."

Carole was looking around the stall, checking to make sure everything was done. "Fresh water—check. Hay—check. Feet cleaned—check," she murmured.

Meanwhile, Lisa had moved closer to the front of the stall and cocked her head to one side. "Uh-oh," she whispered. "Snob alert." She had just heard the loud, familiar sound of Veronica's voice coming from her horse's stall, which was a short distance down the stable row.

Stevie groaned. "Just what I need," she said. "Are Tessa and Phil there, too? Maybe we can lure them to safety."

"I don't hear them," Lisa reported. She crept to the front of the stall, still listening. She frowned. "Actually, they must not be there. I think Veronica's talking about them."

"Who's she talking to?" Carole asked.

Stevie hurried forward to join Lisa at the front of Starlight's stall. "Never mind that," she muttered. "What's she *saying*?"

The three girls listened in silence for a moment. Veronica's voice sounded a bit hoarse, as though she were trying to whisper but was too excited to remember to keep quiet. Her words floated toward them clearly over the other sounds of the stable.

". . . so I think she likes him," she said. "As in *likes* him likes him."

"Really?" someone else asked with a giggle.

"Betsy Cavanaugh," Lisa whispered, identifying the second voice.

Stevie didn't reply. She leaned forward, still trying to hear.

"Definitely," Veronica went on. "I mean, I totally felt like a third wheel in the tack room just now. I finally decided to take her not-so-subtle hints and leave the two of them alone." She snorted. "I was glad to do it, though, believe me. If you ask me, this is the best thing that could happen to either of them."

"How come?" Betsy asked breathlessly. "Do you think he likes her back?"

"Oh, I'm sure of it," Veronica replied, sounding pleased. "I'd swear I saw him wink at Tessa a couple of times." She laughed. "I think it's adorable. Maybe Phil is finally waking up and getting some taste!"

STEVIE FELT AS though her head were going to explode. "How dare she!" she cried, rushing toward the aisle. "I'm going to—*mmmpf*." The last part came out as a muffled but indignant squawk as Lisa grabbed her by the arm and Carole clapped a hand over her mouth to silence her.

"Hush!" Carole hissed. "You don't want Veronica to know you heard her, do you?"

Stevie shoved her hand away. "Hey!" she said, spitting a small piece of hay into the corner of the stall. "You could at least wash your hands before you do that." She glanced at the aisle with a frown, though Lisa was still holding her back. "Anyway, who says I don't want her to hear me? I think she has a right to know why I'm going to throttle her."

"Get real, Stevie," Lisa said. "Since when do you believe Veronica's silly gossip? She made the whole thing up. I mean, come on. This is Phil we're talking about." She hesitated for a split second before adding, "And Tessa. Neither one of them would ever do anything like that."

Stevie thought about that. "Well, Tessa has been acting awfully weird lately," she muttered. She sighed. "But I guess you're right. I trust Phil." She clenched her fists. "Still, why would Veronica make up something like that?"

Carole shrugged. "Why does Veronica do anything?" she asked philosophically. "She's probably just trying to start gossip and make trouble. As usual."

"Or maybe she's just trying to get out of cleaning all that sweaty tack," Lisa suggested. "This way she can make Tessa and Phil do all the work and still take credit for it with Mrs. Pennington—and Miles, of course." In the past few days it had been obvious that Veronica's crush on Miles hadn't faded one bit.

"Hmmm." Stevie was silent for a moment. She knew her friends were right. So why did she still have the urge to rush straight to the tack room and find out for herself what was going on? "All right," she said casually. "Well, since Veronica abandoned them with all that tack to clean, maybe we should go help them out."

Lisa rolled her eyes. "All right," she said. "I guess we could do that."

The girls left Starlight's stall and headed down the

aisle. Stevie gritted her teeth as she realized that Veronica was still whispering about Tessa and Phil.

". . . so I bet they're smooching in there right now," Veronica was saying gleefully. "I could see it in their eyes . . ."

Stevie forced herself to stop listening. "Come on," she said, hurrying around the corner at the end of the stable aisle.

She almost barreled into Max, who had just come out of the locker room. "Whoa," he said. "What do I always tell you about running in the stable?"

"I wasn't running," Stevie protested immediately. "Just walking fast."

Lisa elbowed her in the ribs. "Um, what Stevie meant to say is 'Sorry, Max. It won't happen again,' " she said.

Max frowned. "All right, then," he said. "Since you girls seem to have so much energy, why don't you go help with Hodge and Podge? Red and Miles cooled them out, but they still need grooming. And their stalls could probably use cleaning."

Stevie glanced at the tack room door, which was shut. She opened her mouth to protest. Then she noticed the look in Max's eye and remembered that The Saddle Club was still on probation. "Sure, Max," she said meekly. "We'd be glad to help out."

It seemed to take hours to make the Cleveland Bays comfortable, though with all three girls and Miles working together, it actually took less than half an hour. Finally The Saddle Club was free to return to the previous order of business.

"Do you think they're still in there?" Carole asked as she and her friends approached the tack room door, which was still closed. "What could be taking them so long?" Realizing what she had said and what it could mean, she glanced at Stevie and gulped. "Oops," she said quickly. "I mean, they had a lot of tack to clean."

Lisa shot her a dirty look. Then she smiled tentatively at Stevie. "Okay," she said, her voice a little too cheerful. "Well, let's see if Phil is ready to head over to TD's."

Before the three girls could step closer, the door suddenly flew open. Tessa and Phil rushed into the aisle, looking at each other and giggling. As soon as they noticed the three girls standing there, they immediately stopped laughing.

"Oh, um, hi," Phil stammered, his face turning red.

Stevie glared at him. "Hello," she said evenly. "Is the tack all clean and shiny?"

"Oh, yes." Tessa's cheeks were pink, too, but she was still smiling. "Everything's under control. *Completely* under control."

Carole stared at her. Then she glanced at Phil. He was staring at his feet. He glanced over at Tessa, then turned away and started whistling. Carole wasn't sure what to think. What was going on? She glanced at Stevie and

Lisa. She could tell that both of them were just as per-plexed as she was. Could it actually be possible . . .

"Okay, I'm ready," Veronica announced, hurrying up just in time to break up the awkward moment. "Should we go, Tessa? Mrs. Pennington will be waiting for us." She smiled and patted her hair. "I just ran into Miles, and he's going to give us a ride over to his house. He has his own sports car, you know."

"Ready when you are," Tessa said quickly. "I want to look in on Topside before we go, but that won't take a second." She glanced at The Saddle Club. "Right, then," she added brightly. "I'm off. See you later." Within sec-onds, she and Veronica had disappeared around the cor-ner in the direction of Topside's stall.

Phil had returned to examining the floor. "Uh, listen," he said at last. "Would you guys mind if we did the TD's thing another time? Um, I just remembered some stuff I'm supposed to do at home."

Stevie crossed her arms over her chest and stared at him. "Fine," she replied, her voice icy. "Suddenly I'm not in the mood for ice cream anyway."

Phil looked a bit surprised at her tone. He seemed about to speak, then shrugged instead. "Okay," he said. "See you." He scurried down the aisle toward the exit.

When he was gone, Lisa gave Stevie a worried look. "Are you all right?" she asked uncertainly. "I mean, we don't really know—"

"I'm fine," Stevie snapped. "I mean, anger is a healthy emotion, right? So I'm probably the healthiest person in the state of Virginia right about now."

Carole gulped. "Um, okay," she said. "Does this mean none of us are going to TD's today?"

"I told you," Stevie said. "I'm not in the mood."

"To be honest, I'm not either," Lisa confessed. "I really ought to get home and see if my mom's gone completely mental yet because of the new event."

Carole nodded, feeling slightly relieved. As much as she would have liked to have a Saddle Club meeting and get to the bottom of this whole mess, she had the funniest feeling it wasn't going to happen that day. She had rarely seen Stevie look so angry. And Lisa was already glancing distractedly at her watch.

"Okay," she said. "Let's check on the horses one last time. Then we can all walk out together. We'll meet back here in ten minutes, okay?"

"Got it," Lisa said. Stevie just nodded and let out something that sounded suspiciously like a growl.

Carole was the first one to arrive back at the meeting spot. She leaned against the wall and stared at the tack room door, now standing half open. Could Veronica have been right? Could something be going on between Tessa and Phil? It just didn't seem possible. No matter how Carole looked at it, she simply couldn't believe that either one of them would ever do something like that.

Then she remembered the expressions on their faces

when they had emerged from the tack room. Both of them had seemed almost giddy. Not to mention secretive . . .

"Ready to go?" Lisa asked, hurrying over. "Where's Stevie?"

Carole snapped out of her unsettling thoughts. "Not here yet."

"Yes I am," Stevie replied, rounding the corner from the stable aisle at that moment. "Let's get out of here."

"Hold on," Lisa said. "Prancer slobbered all over me when I was giving her some carrots. Just let me stop in the tack room and wash my hands."

Carole and Stevie nodded and followed Lisa into the tack room. Once they all got a look at the scene inside, they gasped.

"What on earth happened in here?" Carole cried, staring in dismay.

The place was a mess. Normally Max and his riders kept the tack room in a sort of chaotic orderliness. Saddles, bridles, and other tack and equipment were everywhere, but like all the riders at Pine Hollow, Carole knew that once you learned the system, you realized that each item, no matter how small, had its own place. You also learned that you had better make sure each item was returned to its proper spot after use. Max didn't appreciate sloppiness, and he didn't hesitate to let you know it.

Carole could hardly imagine what Max would say if he saw his tack room right then. Half a dozen saddles had been pushed off their racks onto the floor. One was even stuffed into the large concrete sink in the corner of the room. Bridles had been flung in a pile against one wall and looked hopelessly tangled together. A bucket full of spare bits had been tipped over and its contents scattered across the floor. And a couple of turnout rugs that had been neatly folded on a shelf the last time Carole saw them were draped carelessly over a trunk, their ends dragging on the dusty floor.

"Wow," Lisa said, gazing around wide-eyed. "This is—I mean—Wow."

Carole knew what she meant. In all her years at Pine Hollow, she had never seen such a mess. "What happened here?" she asked. "Could someone have done this by accident? A new rider, maybe, or a guest who didn't know any better? Someone's dog?"

Stevie shook her head grimly. "It would have to be some accident," she said. "It looks like a tornado hit this place. Even a Great Dane couldn't do this much damage in the time we've been gone."

"That's right," Lisa remembered. "We were just here ten minutes ago, and this place was fine." Suddenly she frowned. "Or was it?" she added. "Actually, we didn't come in when we were here before."

Carole shrugged. "Yeah, but Tessa and Phil did," she said. "And no matter how weird they were acting, they definitely would have noticed if—" She let out a horrified gasp. "Oh no!" she cried. "You—You don't think *they* did this, do you?"

"No way," Lisa said immediately. "They're not that irresponsible." She gulped. "Of course, they were kind of distracted. And neither one of them has spent all that much time in our tack room. If it was already a little messy when they got there . . . and they bumped into a few things while they were moving around . . ."

"They may have been too busy gazing into each other's eyes to notice," Stevie finished for her, her own eyes flashing fire. She ran both hands through her hair, glaring at the messy room. "This stinks," she said fiercely. "It really stinks."

"No kidding," Lisa agreed. She glanced at her watch. "We don't have time to deal with this right now. But if Max finds it, someone is going to be in big trouble."

Stevie nodded grimly. "And if he finds out we were here and didn't do anything about it, even if it wasn't our fault—"

"We're history," Carole finished, drawing one finger across her throat. "We can kiss our horses good-bye for the rest of the summer."

Stevie bent down and grabbed a handful of the scattered bits. "I can't believe this," she muttered, flinging them across the room in the general direction of the overturned bucket. "This is so unfair!"

Carole gulped. She could tell that Stevie was in no

mood for cleaning right then. She was too angry, and that was making her just as careless as Tessa and Phil must have been. In fact, although a few of the bits she had thrown had actually landed in or near the bucket, several others had missed completely and slid under the sink, where they would be even harder to retrieve.

"Wait," Carole said, putting a hand on Stevie's arm as she bent to grab another handful of bits. "There's no sense in all of us having to hang around and deal with this." She took a deep breath and quickly surveyed the room once more. "This mess really isn't as bad as it looks," she said. "I can take care of it myself."

"Don't be silly," Lisa protested quickly. "We'll all pitch in. Right, Stevie?"

Stevie nodded distractedly and kicked at one of the saddles on the floor.

"No, really," Carole said. "You need to go home and deal with your mom, right?"

"Well . . . sort of," Lisa admitted reluctantly, sneaking another glance at her watch.

"And Stevie, you really don't want to hang around this tack room right now, do you?" Carole added.

Stevie shrugged. "That's the understatement of the year," she muttered.

"But you shouldn't have to do all this work yourself," Lisa said.

Carole started pushing her toward the door. Stevie

trailed along behind. "Don't worry about it," Carole said. "I'll be fine. In fact, I'll probably get done faster without a couple of distracted best friends in the way." She smiled.

Lisa smiled back. "Well, if you're sure . . . Thanks," she said gratefully. "We'll make it up to you next time."

Stevie nodded. "Definitely." She gave Carole a brief smile before her scowl returned. Then she headed for the door, muttering under her breath.

Carole and Lisa exchanged worried glances. Still, Carole knew that there wasn't much they could do to help Stevie right then—other than trying to figure out what was going on. She would cool down in her own time. "See you tomorrow," Carole said.

Lisa took one last look around the tack room. "Good luck," she told Carole.

"Thanks," Carole replied. "Same to you."

When her friends were gone, Carole glanced around the room with a sigh. "First things first," she muttered, grabbing the saddle out of the sink. She had to at least make things look marginally presentable in case Max or Red happened by. That meant picking up the saddles and bridles and shaking out and folding the turnout rugs. After that, she could start on the more minor stuff, like picking up the bits and cleaning the tack that had been on the floor.

She sighed. Despite what she had told her friends, this was going to be a real pain in the neck.

* * *

By the time the tack room was spic-and-span once again, Carole's mood was almost as bad as Stevie's.

"There," she muttered, hanging the last perfectly clean bridle on its assigned rack and stretching out her tired hands and shoulders. "All done." *And if I ever find out who was responsible for this*, she thought grimly, *Stevie will have to stand in line behind me to throttle him. Or her. Or them.*

She still had a hard time believing that Tessa or Phil could have had anything to do with this. Normally she would have assumed that Veronica was the culprit. But this time, she had to admit, all the evidence seemed to point to her friends. A toddler or small child couldn't have done it—the turnout rugs and some of the tack had been placed too high for a child to reach. A canine vandal seemed unlikely, since there were no tooth marks in any of the leather. Who else could be responsible, then, but a completely distracted couple paying more attention to each other than to what they were doing?

Carole sighed. Her head ached, and she didn't feel like thinking about this anymore. She needed a distraction. Luckily, she knew just where to find one.

"Hey, boy," she said gently, slipping into Starlight's stall a moment later. The horse greeted her with a soft nicker, and Carole smiled for the first time in hours.

A few minutes later she reluctantly patted Starlight good-bye and left his stall. It was getting late, and she knew her father would be expecting her. Besides, her brief visit with her horse had made her feel much better already. Horses had a way of doing that. It had always been that way—for Carole, at least. It made her feel very sorry for all the people who didn't have daily access to horses.

She headed down the aisle, enjoying the quiet sounds of the stable around her. Everyone else seemed to have left, so all she could hear were the pleasant noises made by contented horses—the chewing of hay, the slurping of water, the occasional snort or nicker . . .

Suddenly Carole heard a sound that didn't belong.

Clang! Clang!

She frowned. "What was that?" she muttered.

Clang!

She hurried forward, heading in the direction of the noise. It sounded an awful lot like a hoof hitting metal.

Clang! Clang!

Carole followed the sound to Topside's stall. When she looked inside, she immediately spotted the problem. A large metal bucket was lying on its side in the back corner of the stall. Topside, a naturally curious horse, was kicking at it experimentally with his front hoof.

"Topside," Carole called to the gelding, forcing her voice to stay calm and soothing. She opened the stall door and stepped inside. "Here, boy. Come up here."

The horse turned at the sound of her voice. He nickered eagerly and hurried forward to greet her, nosing her hands and pockets for treats.

Carole found a stray piece of carrot in her pocket and

fed it to him. Then she walked to the back of the stall and picked up the bucket.

"How did this get in here?" she muttered. She glanced at the spot partway up the back wall where Topside's flat-backed plastic water bucket usually hung. The hook was empty, and the plastic bucket was nowhere in sight.

Carole was starting to figure out what might have happened, and she didn't like it one bit. She stuck her hand into the metal bucket and found a few drops of water still inside. Glancing at the floor, she saw that the straw bedding was wet where the bucket had been lying.

She took a deep breath, trying to stay calm for the horse's sake. "It's okay, Topside," she said, giving the big gelding a pat on the shoulder. "I'll go get you some nice fresh water. Don't worry."

She let herself out of the stall. As she hurried back to the tack room, she felt her fury growing uncontrollably. She knew that if she hadn't found the metal bucket when she did, Topside could have stepped in it and injured himself badly—maybe even broken a leg. That was why Max used plastic buckets to water the horses, and why even those were always to be attached firmly to the wall rather than left loose. Leaving a metal bucket on the floor went beyond carelessness: It practically guaranteed trouble. Only the most careless, ignorant, or malicious rider would have done such a thing.

Carole's hands were shaking as she grabbed a plastic

bucket from the stack in the tack room and filled it at the sink. Who could have done this?

Tessa. Her mind piped up with the obvious answer, though Carole did her best to shove it away. *Tessa must have done it. Tessa rides Topside. Tessa was in his stall just before she left. Tessa is careless. Tessa left the tack room a mess . . .*

Carole took a deep breath, trying to find another explanation, but she couldn't. As impossible as it was to believe that Tessa could have left the bucket there, it was even more ridiculous to imagine that Max or Red could have done it. And who else could it have been?

LISA GLANCED AT the phone on the kitchen wall for about the thousandth time, wondering if she should call Carole or Stevie. She had been working nonstop ever since arriving home from the stable. At the moment, she was sitting at the kitchen table surrounded by signs, lists, charts, receipts, reference books, and who knew what else. Her mother had just left for the store to buy some more supplies and pick up more information at Mrs. diAngelo's house, which meant even more work when she returned.

Lisa sighed and tore her gaze away from the phone. Doing all this work was bad enough, but doing it all alone made it even more tedious. It was tempting to call her friends to help, but she just couldn't do it. Not after what had happened that day. She suspected that Carole was probably still trying to sort out the mess in the tack room—and if she wasn't, she was certainly too exhausted from all the extra work to want to start collating phone lists. As for Stevie . . . Lisa shuddered. Somehow she didn't think Stevie was in any mood to deal with Mrs. Atwood right now. She was far too distracted by her suspicions about Phil. It might have been different if Lisa could have honestly reassured her. But she had to admit that things just didn't look good where Phil and Tessa were concerned.

Speaking of Tessa . . . Lisa checked the clock on the microwave. It would have been nice if Tessa had come home to help. After all, adding a new event to the point-to-point had been her idea. Instead, she seemed to be planning to spend the whole day with Veronica—again. She hadn't so much as called since the two of them had left with Miles.

Lisa sighed. There wasn't much she could do about that, so she vowed to stop thinking about it. She didn't have time, anyway—not if she wanted to finish all the tasks her mother had assigned her before she came home and handed out even more. Lisa grabbed the layout of the program in one hand and a dictionary in the other. "Back to proofreading," she muttered to herself.

"YOU KNOW, I hate to admit it," Carole commented to
Stevie and Lisa the next day, "but I'm actually kind of
glad that Tessa decided to go on that trail ride with Veronica."

"I don't hate to admit it at all," Stevie replied, swinging Belle's empty water bucket at her side as the three
girls left the tack room together. "I'm definitely glad. By
the way, Lisa, are you absolutely, positively sure that Tessa
didn't make any phone calls last night?"

Lisa frowned. "I'm sure." She knew that Stevie was
worried that Tessa might have called Phil. But on this
point, at least, Lisa could reassure her. "Like I told you,
she was positively *exhausted* when she got home from dinner at Veronica's place last night." The words came out

sounding more sarcastic than she'd intended, but she couldn't quite make herself feel guilty about it. "She went straight to bed," she went on. "Never mind that Mom and I were up half the night working on the point-to-point."

Carole didn't seem to be listening. She was staring down at Starlight's water bucket, which she was carrying. "Listen, you guys," she said. "If you don't mind, I think we should stop by Topside's stall to make sure everything is okay."

Stevie shrugged. "Why?" she asked. "He's not there. Tessa has him out on the trail, remember?"

"I know." Carole hesitated. "I just want to check, that's all."

Lisa nodded. Carole had told her and Stevie about the incident with the water bucket. She really couldn't blame her for being worried. "Okay," she said. "Let's meet there in fifteen minutes."

EXACTLY FIFTEEN MINUTES later, Stevie poked her head over the half door of Topside's stall. "Uh-oh," she muttered.

Carole and Lisa walked up at that moment. "Uh-oh what?" Carole asked. "What's wrong this time?"

"Take a look for yourself," Stevie said, stepping back to give her friends room. "Or rather, take a *smell*."

The others immediately saw the problem. Topside's stall clearly hadn't been mucked out in hours. Clumps of manure were everywhere. "Oh no." Carole sighed. "I guess Tessa decided to wait to muck out when she got back from her ride."

"If she plans to do it at all," Stevie muttered.

Lisa shook her head in dismay. "We can't leave it like this," she said, wrinkling her nose at the dirty, matted bedding. "If Max sees it, he'll have a cow."

"Great," Stevie said. "Maybe Tessa would take better care of a cow."

Carole gulped. Stevie and Lisa sounded really angry with Tessa. She couldn't really blame them. It seemed that every time they turned around these days, Tessa was causing extra work. Carole knew that Lisa hadn't gotten to sleep until very late the night before. And she suspected that Stevie hadn't slept much better—she had probably been up half the night brooding about Tessa and Phil.

Carole was angry herself at the thought that Tessa could have been responsible for the mess in the tack room the day before—and especially for that loose water bucket in Topside's stall. And now Tessa seemed to have left another mess that would have to be cleaned up by her friends.

Still, something was bothering Carole about this whole situation. How could they have misjudged Tessa so completely? Back in England—and even last week here in Virginia, for that matter—Tessa had seemed just as responsible and hardworking as any of them. She had pitched in willingly to do her own work and help with everyone else's. Carole had thought she knew the British girl. She had trusted her. Could she really have been so wrong?

She thought about it as she worked beside her friends to clean out the dirty stall. But she couldn't come up with any good explanation for Tessa's behavior.

She was rolling a wheelbarrow full of droppings and dirty straw out of Topside's stall when she suddenly noticed something. She stopped and frowned down at her cargo. "Hey, you guys," she called. "Did you notice anything strange about this manure?"

Lisa poked her head out of the stall. "What did you say?"

Carole carefully backed up and stopped the wheelbarrow in the open stall door. "Check it out," she said. "It looks kind of dark. And soft, or something."

Stevie, broom in hand, glanced at the wheelbarrow and made a face. "Come on, Carole," she complained. "It's almost lunchtime. Do we really have to study Topside's manure right now?"

Carole shrugged, still feeling bothered by the unusual texture. "Sorry," she said. "It just looks kind of weird . . ."

"Don't worry about it," Lisa said a bit impatiently, leaning on the handle of the shovel she was using. "I'm sure the manure is fine. You're just looking for trouble because—well, you know."

Carole shrugged again. She glanced down at the soiled

straw, wondering if Lisa was right. Topside's manure really didn't look *that* strange. Still . . .

Lisa noticed her hesitation. "Look," she said. "We can check on Topside later, okay? If you still think there might be something wrong, we'll tell Max."

"Okay," Carole agreed, feeling a little bit better. She picked up the handles of the wheelbarrow and started down the aisle toward the back door of the stable.

When she returned from her trip to the muck heap, Stevie and Lisa were talking about the scurry race. "We were just saying it might be fun to enter a team in the race," Lisa told Carole.

Carole nodded. "I was thinking that, too," she said, glad her friends had changed the subject. She was tired of talking and thinking about Tessa, Phil, and Veronica. "And since the event was added at the last minute, it probably won't attract nearly enough really good scurry teams like the Penningtons' . . ."

Stevie grinned, guessing what Carole was thinking. "So even a bunch of rank beginners like us might have a chance to land in the ribbons," she said. "That decides it. Let's do it!"

Lisa, too, seemed relieved at the change of subject. "Do you think Max would let us use his pony cart?" she asked.

"Sure." Stevie shrugged. "Why not? He's not *that* mad at us."

"Which horses would we use, though?" Carole asked worriedly. "None of ours are trained to harness, and that's a pretty specialized thing. There's no way we could get them ready before Saturday. . . ."

"I think we should use ponies," Lisa said. Besides the horses ridden by the older riders, Max kept some ponies for younger children to ride during lessons. "Most of them are trained to pull a cart. We've seen them do it lots of times. And remember, Mrs. Pennington said it was okay to enter ponies so long as you have a pair."

"Perfect!" Stevie grinned. "Besides, smaller horses will be an advantage. They'll be able to turn quicker and be less likely to run into the cones."

The girls continued to discuss their scurry team as they finished working on Topside's stall. When they were finished, they headed toward the office to find Max.

"Just pray he says yes," Lisa said, crossing her fingers. "After all, we're still on probation."

But instead of Max, they found his mother, known to one and all as Mrs. Reg. She was seated behind the desk working on some papers.

"Hello, girls," she said as they knocked and entered. She listened quietly to their request. Then she smiled. "I can't say this is a complete surprise," she said. "Max warned me you might come along and ask something like this."

"And?" Carole held her breath.

Mrs. Reg chuckled. "And it's fine," she said. "Consider yourselves the official Pine Hollow scurry team."

* * *

"WHOA, NICKEL!" STEVIE called in frustration forty-five minutes later. "Can't you tell your left from your right?"

Carole giggled as the sweet-faced gray pony turned to give Stevie a look of reproachful surprise. "I think he's saying he knows left from right very well," she joked from her seat beside Stevie. "He just can't tell which you want when you have his reins and Dime's all twisted up like that."

Stevie had to laugh, too, as she glanced down at the four reins she was trying to keep straight in her hands. "This driving stuff isn't as easy as it looks," she admitted ruefully.

"No," Lisa said, leaning forward from the backseat of the pony cart. "But it's fun, isn't it?"

Both her friends had to agree with that. Scurry driving definitely wasn't easy, but it *was* fun. Best of all, it was actually taking their minds off their other problems.

Lisa shaded her eyes with one hand and peered over the fence of the outdoor ring to the fields beyond. "Look," she said. "I think Tessa and Veronica are finally coming back from their trail ride."

"Hmmm," Carole responded. She glanced at her friends. "Am I the only one who's thinking maybe we were a little too hard on her before?"

"Yes," Stevie said quickly. But she immediately looked guilty. "Well, no," she admitted. "I was sort of wondering the same thing. After all, the law is still 'innocent until proven guilty.'" Both of Stevie's parents were lawyers, so they were always saying things like that. This time, Stevie thought they might be right. They couldn't write off Tessa completely until they found out for sure what was going on, no matter how suspicious things looked.

Lisa nodded. "I guess you're right." She took a deep breath of the fresh summer air and glanced at the approaching riders. "Come on, I think the ponies have had enough for today. Let's take them in and then see if Tessa needs any help with Topside."

"THERE YOU GO, boy," Tessa said cheerfully, snapping the hook shut on the handle of Topside's plastic water bucket. She patted the horse fondly on his well-groomed flank, then left the stall to join Carole in the aisle.

Carole smiled. She had watched Tessa's every move carefully, and she had to admit that Tessa had taken perfect care of the horse ever since arriving back at the stable after her trail ride. In fact, things almost seemed to be back to normal, except for the minor unpleasant fact that Tessa had agreed to have dinner at Veronica's house that evening. Still, Carole supposed, that could have been written off to good manners.

"Stevie and Lisa should be finished grooming the ponies by now," she said. "But we still have to clean their tack. Want to join us?"

"Absolutely," Tessa replied with a grin, hoisting Topside's saddle onto one shoulder. "Topside really worked up a sweat out on the trail—Veronica and I did some jumping so that she could practice for the junior hurdle. This tack will need a right good scrubbing today."

Carole smiled again. This was more like it. Whatever had happened the day before, the *real* Tessa seemed to be back.

The two girls found Lisa and Stevie already at work in the tack room. Soon all four of them were busy cleaning tack, chatting as they worked. Tessa told them about the meeting with Mrs. Pennington the day before.

"She's really eager to help," she said. "It's obvious she's mad for scurry racing and all sorts of driving, and she wants everyone else to love it as much as she does." She looked up from Topside's bridle and winked. "Plus, it didn't hurt that Miles hung around the entire time we were there." She blushed and giggled. "I know he's a bit older, but I'm starting to fancy him a bit. He's rather cute, don't you think?"

"Definitely." Stevie smiled. This was good news. If Tessa had her eye on Miles, that meant the scene with Phil yesterday must have been all a big mistake.

"Anyway," Tessa went on, "now that I've got to know Miles better, it makes me feel happier about being a fence judge on Saturday." She grinned and stopped working to gaze steadily at her friends for a moment. "Actually, I can't wait. The point-to-point is going to be wonderful." Her eyes danced gleefully. "I can positively guarantee it."

"You don't have to convince us," Stevie replied happily. She was already wondering if Phil had noticed that she was mad at him the day before. She hoped not. Maybe she would call him that night to make sure. "We're totally psyched. Especially now that we're entering the scurry race."

"Oh, yes," Tessa said with a short laugh. "I just know the scurry race is going to be the best of all."

Lisa looked up from the breast collar she was cleaning. Something about Tessa's voice sounded a little strange.

"Anyway," Tessa said brightly, "I was just thinking— do you suppose we could have another sleepover on Friday night? You know, so we can talk about the point-to-point and everything." She shot Lisa a sympathetic glance. "Also, it might help if we were all there to help keep Lisa's mum as calm as possible."

Lisa smiled at her gratefully. "That's a fantastic idea." She could hardly believe Tessa would be so thoughtful as to think of that. No, actually she *could* believe it. What she could hardly believe was that she'd ever doubted Tessa. "Let's do it."

8

"Hi, Mrs. Marsten," Stevie said into the phone that evening after dinner. "It's Stevie. Is Phil there?"

"Stevie?" Phil's mother paused. "What do you mean, dear? Phil's not here."

Stevie was disappointed. She still felt a bit guilty about her earlier suspicions. She had hoped to talk to Phil and make sure he hadn't noticed anything. It would be terrible if the two of them were at odds for any reason right before the point-to-point. "Oh, too bad," she said to Mrs. Marsten. She leaned back on her bed. "Um, do you know what time he'll be back?"

There was another pause. "I'm sorry," Mrs. Marsten said at last. "Who did you say this was?"

"It's me," Stevie replied, surprised. "Stevie. Stevie Lake."

"Now I'm really confused," Mrs. Marsten said. "Stevie, Phil isn't here. He left an hour ago—he asked his sister to drive him over to Willow Creek. I naturally assumed he was coming to see you."

"Oh." Stevie thought about that for a second. She didn't like what it implied. She didn't like it one bit. "Um, okay. Thanks anyway."

"Shall I ask him to call you when he gets in?" Mrs. Marsten asked.

"No, no," Stevie said quickly. "That's okay. Actually, you don't even have to tell him I called. Bye."

She hung up and set the phone back on her bedside table. All her earlier suspicions were back, and then some. What was going on? Why would Phil want to come to Willow Creek unless it was to see her?

To see someone else. That much was obvious. Unfortunately, there was also one very obvious person he might want to see . . . "Don't be stupid," Stevie muttered to herself. "Lisa would tell me if Phil showed up over there."

That made her feel slightly better. But she was still bothered by the situation. She decided to go downstairs and make herself a snack. Maybe that would cheer her up.

She walked into the kitchen. Her older brother, Chad, and her twin brother, Alex, were seated at the table gobbling down the remains of a chocolate cake.

"Hey," Stevie said, snatching the platter away just as

Alex was about to spear the last slice with his fork. "Save some for the rest of us, will you?" She grabbed the cake without bothering to get a plate and took a big bite.

Chad rolled his eyes. "Really, Stevie," he said, swallowing his mouthful of cake. "Haven't any of Tessa's manners rubbed off on you?"

Alex laughed. "Yeah, really," he added teasingly. "How can you hang out with someone like her and still act the way you do? I mean, she's a real lady. And you're more of a . . ." He paused, obviously searching for just the right comparison.

"A horse?" Chad suggested helpfully.

Alex shook his head. "No, I was thinking more along the lines of a gorilla."

Stevie rolled her eyes as her brothers snorted with laughter. "Ha, ha," she said heavily. The last thing she felt like doing right then was getting into a discussion about how wonderful Tessa was. "So is there any milk left, or did you warthogs down all of that, too?" She walked over to the refrigerator to check.

Her brothers weren't finished. "You know, Stevie," Chad said, sounding just a little too casual, "I have another intramural baseball game on Friday night. Maybe Tessa would like to come and watch like she did last week."

Stevie froze in her tracks. This was too much. She recognized the tone in her brother's voice. It was the tone that meant he had yet another crush on yet another girl.

And this time, it seemed, the girl was Tessa. She gritted her teeth. "I don't think so," she replied evenly. "We're having a sleepover on Friday night."

"Too bad," Alex said gleefully. "Hey, Stevie, how much longer is Tessa going to be here, anyway? Maybe if we asked nicely, Mom and Dad would take us all to King's Dominion or Busch Gardens. Tessa, too," he added quickly.

"Hey, that would be a blast," Chad agreed eagerly. "Tessa seems like the kind of girl who'd have fun riding roller coasters and stuff."

Alex nodded. "Yeah. She seems pretty cool. You know, for a horse freak."

Stevie groaned and set the remains of her cake down on the counter. Suddenly her appetite had vanished. Obviously Tessa's friendly personality and exotic accent had completely won over her brothers. Just the way it had won over Phil . . .

"Give it up," Stevie told her brothers sourly. "You don't know anything about Tessa." *I'm beginning to wonder how well any of us really knows her*, she thought grimly. *For instance, who could have predicted that she'd suddenly want to become best friends with Veronica diAngelo?*

Suddenly Stevie gasped. She had just remembered something—something that made her forget all about her annoying brothers. Tessa wasn't at Lisa's house this evening. She was having dinner with Veronica!

Or maybe Veronica is just covering for her, Stevie thought as a cold, tight fist seemed to clutch at her heart. *Maybe she's* really *spending this evening with Phil!*

A TROUBLED FROWN creased Carole's brow as she paged through a well-worn reference book about equine health. She had already checked all the entries having to do with manure about a dozen times, but she still couldn't stop thinking about Topside. What if there really was something wrong with him?

She tried to reassure herself. Aside from the slightly odd-looking extra-large load of manure she had noticed that day, there didn't seem to be a single thing different about the gelding's appearance or behavior. If there had been, Max or Red would have noticed and called the vet. Still, the question about the odd-looking droppings had been nagging at her all evening.

Max counts on the riders to check their horses carefully, Carole fretted. *And he thinks Tessa is a totally responsible rider . . .*

She sighed and closed the book. Staring at the surface of her desk, she ran back over the last few days in her mind. Tessa had been awfully busy with Veronica lately. Could that have distracted her enough to make her make all those mistakes—the tack, the water bucket, the dirty stall?

Worse yet, Carole thought, could it be that they were only now seeing Tessa's true personality emerging? Maybe she wasn't as nice and smart and responsible as they had thought. Maybe she had just been on her best behavior before—and now that she had found a more compatible friend in Veronica, she was finally letting her true colors shine through. How well did they really know her, after all?

Carole sighed and opened the book to the index again. Would they ever figure out the truth?

LISA CLICKED ON the Save icon with the mouse on her family's computer and sat back in her chair while the machine hummed away. She rubbed her eyes, which were tired from staring at the screen for the past two hours. She had just put the finishing touches on the program for the point-to-point. Now all she had to do was save it onto a separate disk so that her mother could take it to the printer's office the next day.

At least she can manage to do that, Lisa thought grump-ily. But she immediately felt bad. It really wasn't her mother's fault that she couldn't work the computer very well. And Lisa had volunteered to take care of the pro-gram—mostly because she was sick to death of painting Parking and No Parking signs, which was the other big job that remained. Lisa had also felt responsible for the changes that had to be made in the program because of the addition of the scurry race. After all, it had been her friend's idea to add the new event.

Of course, it would be nice if Tessa were here to help out, Lisa thought. And this time she didn't feel the least bit bad about the thought. She glanced at her watch. Tessa had been with Veronica all day. Lisa couldn't imagine what they were doing.

But she knew what Tessa *wasn't* doing: helping. And wasn't that what The Saddle Club was supposed to be about? Maybe they had been premature, asking Tessa to join when they really didn't know her very well. Lisa knew that if she had called Stevie or Carole anytime this afternoon and asked them to come over and help out, they would have done it if they could. In fact, she had thought about doing just that more than once. But she had held back. She told herself it was because they had other things on their minds. But deep down, she knew the real reason: She felt too guilty. After all, she was the one who had first introduced them to Tessa . . .

9

"Ooh, Veronica, you were right!" Tessa called across the outdoor ring. "Danny's trot is heavenly!"

"I told you." Veronica looked smug. "He's a dream, isn't he? Oh, but of course Topside has his good points, too."

"Gag," Lisa whispered as she watched the scene. It was the next day, and since Friday would be spent getting ready for the point-to-point, they were having their riding lesson a day early. "I can't believe Max actually agreed to let them switch horses today."

Carole shrugged. "I can," she said, loosening Starlight's reins slightly as he stretched his head to sniff at a clod of dirt. "He's always saying it's good practice to ride different

108

horses sometimes. I'm just surprised he didn't die of shock when Veronica suggested it. Usually she won't let anyone come within five feet of Danny without pitching a fit."

"Not true," Stevie corrected quickly. "She's happy to let Red near him—as long as he's grooming him or cleaning his stall or feeding him—"

"Okay, okay," Carole said with a rueful smile. "We get the picture!"

Stevie glanced at Tessa and Veronica again, who were now riding side by side at the other end of the ring. The two girls had their heads tilted close together and seemed to be whispering. As Stevie watched, Tessa let out a loud, delighted giggle. Veronica joined in.

"Did you hear that?" Stevie involuntarily tightened her grip on the reins, causing Belle to toss her head. Forcing her hands to relax, Stevie looked at her friends. "I don't trust that giggle. It sounds like a boy-crazy giggle to me. And I think I know which boy they're giggling about." She had already told her friends about her conversation with Phil's mother.

"Just ignore them," Carole suggested lamely. She didn't know what else to say.

A LITTLE LATER THAT day Lisa was in Prancer's stall feeding carrot cubes to the sweet Thoroughbred mare. She had ridden Derby in lessons that day, since the point-to-point was only two days away, and he had performed very well as always. But she was really starting to miss riding Prancer. "Don't worry, girl," she murmured as the mare's soft lips carefully plucked another carrot from her outstretched palm. "We'll go for a nice long trail ride together after the point-to-point is over. I promise."

"Talking to yourself again?" a snotty voice asked from just outside the stall.

Lisa turned and saw Veronica smirking at her. "What do you want?" she asked, in no mood to be polite.

"Just an update for you," Veronica said casually. "I thought I'd let you know so you could call your mother. There's been a slight change in the program."

Lisa gasped. "But there can't be!" she exclaimed. "Mom is supposed to be getting the programs printed up today. It's too late to change it now!"

Veronica shrugged. "Sorry," she said, not sounding sorry at all. "But Tessa had a great idea. She wants to move the scurry race to last on the program instead of having it in the middle of the day. I just called my mother to suggest it to her, and she thinks that will be perfect." She shrugged again. "And she *is* the head of the fundraising committee . . ."

"All right, all right," Lisa grumbled. She gave Prancer one last distracted pat, then headed for the stall door. "I'll call Mom. Maybe she hasn't left yet for the printer's." She crossed her fingers as she said it.

"That's the spirit," Veronica said complacently, stepping back to let her pass. "After all, Tessa's only trying to help. She wants the point-to-point to be as good as it can be. Don't you?"

Lisa didn't bother to reply. She was already rushing for the phone.

CAROLE FINISHED ROLLING a bright red bandage into a neat, tight package and dropped it into the bucket by her feet. Then she leaned over and pulled out another bandage—a blue one this time—from the box perched on the trunk beside her. Alone in the tack room, she was starting to feel as though she lived there these days. This time, she had no one to blame but herself. She had volunteered to roll the boxful of bandages that had been sitting on the edge of Mrs. Reg's desk for almost a week. Even with everything else that was happening around there lately, she hadn't forgotten that The Saddle Club was on probation until Max decided otherwise. And she knew that nothing made him happier than hearing his riders offer to help out with extra stable chores.

As she finished rolling the blue bandage and dropped it into the bucket, Carole heard voices approaching from outside. She looked up, hoping it was Stevie and Lisa. But she frowned when she recognized Veronica's voice.

"So I'm positive that Miles really likes me," she was saying loudly. "He was even hinting around yesterday about my riding with him in the scurry race on Saturday."

"Really?" Carole recognized the second voice as belonging to Betsy Cavanaugh. It sounded as though Betsy and Veronica had paused just outside the tack room door. "That would be so exciting! Is he going to drive Hodge and Podge?"

"No," Veronica replied airily. "He'll be driving their second team. They haven't arrived yet from Pennsylvania, but he arranged specially to have someone drive them down just in time for the point-to-point."

"Are they Cleveland Bays, too?" Betsy asked breathlessly.

Veronica paused. "Um, I don't think so," she said. "He said something about them being a special breed from France. But he didn't go into detail." She giggled in such a self-satisfied way that Carole cringed. "He was too busy telling me how perfect I would look sitting beside him."

"Oh, you would," Betsy assured her.

"I know." Veronica's voice was a little louder. Carole barely had time to grab another bandage and start busily rolling it as the two girls walked into the tack room. "It will be . . ." Her words trailed off as she spotted Carole. "Oh," she said unpleasantly. "I didn't know anyone was in here."

Before Carole could reply, Veronica whirled on her heel and stalked out. Betsy shot Carole an apologetic glance and followed.

Carole snorted in disgust. Obviously she and her friends had completely misjudged Miles Pennington. If he actually liked Veronica as much as she seemed to think he did, he couldn't possibly be as nice as they had thought. *Like some other people I could mention*, Carole thought.

"Hi, Carole," Stevie greeted her, hurrying into the tack room a moment later.

Lisa was right behind her. "What are you doing in here?" she asked.

Carole told them. "I thought it couldn't hurt to volunteer for anything that needs doing around here," she added.

"Good thought." Stevie sat down and grabbed a bright pink bandage out of the box. "I think Max is starting to get over it. But that means this is the critical point. We've got to totally win him over."

Lisa nodded. "Maybe if we're extra helpful through the point-to-point, he'll give in and lift the probation," she said hopefully, reaching into the box. "I mean, how long can he keep on this way?"

Before the others could answer, the door swung open and Veronica and Tessa walked in. "Oh!" Tessa looked surprised when she saw The Saddle Club. "Hi, guys! I didn't know you were in here."

Veronica didn't say anything to the other girls. She just turned to Tessa. "So anyway, as I was saying, I was thinking you could come home with me tomorrow afternoon after we're done here at the stable and spend the night. Wouldn't that be fun?"

Carole bit her lip, remembering that the four of them

had planned a sleepover for the next night. Would Tessa remember? Would she care? Or would she just go off with Veronica without a thought for The Saddle Club?

Tessa looked anxious. "I'm sorry, Veronica," she said. "We're having a slumber party tomorrow at Lisa's house."

Veronica smirked. "Oh, that's right," she said smoothly. "I completely forgot about that. You told me all about it yesterday. It was really nice of you to invite me."

This time Carole heard Lisa and Stevie gasp, too. She couldn't believe her ears. Could this be true? Had Tessa actually invited *Veronica* to a Saddle Club sleepover?

Veronica seemed to be enjoying their reaction. "Don't worry," she said breezily, addressing the three girls at last. "I can't make it to your pathetic little party." She reached over and squeezed Tessa's arm fondly. "But don't worry, Tess. You'll survive it somehow, I'm sure. If you get completely bored, you can call me. I'll be home most of the evening—unless Miles calls, of course. Then you're on your own."

Tessa looked stricken. She glanced from The Saddle Club to Veronica and back again. "Um—" she began.

Veronica cut her off. "So, how about some preparty shopping instead?" she said, addressing Tessa only. "We can pick up a few last-minute things for the point-to-point. I promise to have you back before dinnertime."

"Uh, okay," Tessa said. "That sounds goo—"

"Come on, guys," Stevie said abruptly, standing up so fast that Lisa had to grab the boxful of bandages to keep it

114

from falling off the trunk. "We can finish this later. Let's go practice our jumping for a while. We need to make sure we're in shape for the junior hurdle race."

"Great idea," Carole agreed. She knew they were being rude to Tessa, but for once, she couldn't care less. "It's getting stuffy in here all of a sudden. Let's go."

"DO YOU THINK Tessa knew we were mad at her?" Lisa asked a few minutes later. The three girls had decided to practice for the point-to-point, so they had tacked up their horses and were warming them up by trotting three abreast around the outdoor ring.

Stevie shrugged. "Who cares?" she replied. Her voice was angry. "I can't believe she invited Veronica to a Saddle Club sleepover. What's wrong with her?"

"I don't know." Carole sighed so loudly that Starlight flicked his ears backward. She patted him absently. "It's like she's turned into a totally different person."

"Yeah," Stevie muttered. "A person who likes Veronica diAngelo better than she likes us. It makes me wish she would go spend the night with her new best friend tomorrow." She snorted. "I wish we could cancel the stupid sleepover. The last thing I feel like doing is hanging out with Tessa—Veronica or no Veronica."

"We can't cancel it," Carole replied immediately. "We've got to endure it for Lisa's sake. After all, she's got to put up with Tessa no matter what—and all her mom's last-minute plans."

Stevie nodded. "You're right," she said. "Don't worry, Lisa. We won't abandon you."

"Thanks, guys. I wish I could tell you it's okay not to come." Lisa grimaced. "But I'm not sure I'd survive tomorrow night on my own." She sighed. "Tessa leaves next week. Whoever thought we'd be looking forward to that?"

"I know. It's weird, isn't it?" Carole agreed.

Lisa stopped talking for a moment as Derby tried to break into a prancing canter. "Anyway," she said once she had him under control again, "Tessa aside, I'm not sure the sleepover is going to be much fun. I'm afraid Mom will be hovering over us all night, chattering at Tessa about English steeplechasing and making the rest of us make a million more parking signs."

"It's too bad Max is still mad at us," Stevie said. "Otherwise we could ask him if we could have the sleepover in the loft here at Pine Hollow." The Saddle Club had held several warm-weather sleepovers in the stable's roomy hayloft. She grinned wryly. "But I'm not sure we should be mentioning the hayloft to him right now. It might remind him of the last time we were up there."

Her friends laughed. "It is too bad," Lisa said. "In the loft, without my mom hovering over us every second, we'd be free to ignore Tessa in peace."

"Or maybe find out what's going on with her these days," Carole put in tentatively. She still wondered if all they needed to straighten out this mess was to sit down and have a long talk with Tessa. But a glance at her friends' faces told her that maybe it was too late for that. "But I guess there's no point thinking about it," she added quickly. "Mrs. Atwood would never let Tessa out of her sight for that long."

Lisa laughed wearily. "You're right about that," she agreed. "Come on." She urged Derby into a canter, and the big gelding responded immediately, seeming eager to stretch his legs. "Let's do some jumping!"

Lisa pulled Derby's left ear forward gently. "Steady, boy," she murmured to the horse as he snorted and shifted his feet uneasily. "This will feel good. I promise." She gently brushed the area behind his ear with the soft body brush she was holding. Then she scratched the gelding on his favorite spot on his neck before reaching for his other ear. This time the horse didn't move, though he rolled his eyes back apprehensively.

Carole and Stevie were leaning on the stall door, watching. Normally they would have pitched in to help, but Lisa had asked them not to. She wanted to spend as much time as possible bonding with Derby before the junior hurdle race the next day.

"It's funny how different horses react to things in totally different ways," Stevie remarked. "Belle loves it when I play with her ears. But I guess Derby's sensitive there."

Carole nodded. "They're like people that way," she said. "You know—like some people are ticklish and some aren't."

"Uh-huh," Stevie said. "Or like some people actually seem to enjoy spending all their time at the mall with Veronica diAngelo, and some people would rather have their toenails pulled out one by one and their eyeballs dipped in boiling oil."

Lisa wrinkled her nose. "Ick," she said. "Actually, I'm kind of glad Tessa has been with Veronica all day. It makes it easier to stay away from her."

Stevie nodded sympathetically. "It must have been tough on you last night."

"Not really." Lisa shrugged. "The walk home was a little awkward—Tessa kept trying to pretend that nothing was wrong, but then she kept saying all sorts of things about Veronica and how close and trusting a relationship they have." She turned away from Derby long enough to roll her eyes in disgust. "But Mom put us both to work as soon as we walked in the door, so after that we hardly had time to talk at all. Even if we'd wanted to."

Carole still felt a little unsettled about the situation with Tessa. It seemed sad that a friendship that had started out so wonderfully could have gone astray so quickly. It didn't make sense. She glanced at her watch.

"Hey, we'd better finish up here," she said. "We're sup-posed to meet Tessa back at Lisa's house in less than an hour." The girls had spent part of the afternoon practic-ing for the point-to-point. Afterward, Lisa had decided to give Derby an extra-special grooming while Stevie and Carole took care of their horses.

"Okay," Lisa said. "I'll just be a few more minutes here. Would you mind refilling Derby's water bucket for me?"

"No problem." Stevie stepped into the stall and un-hooked the plastic bucket from its spot on the wall. "I'll be back in a sec."

She headed down the aisle toward the tack room, whistling softly as she went. She was still upset about the situation with Tessa and Phil, but even worrying about that hadn't been able to completely ruin a day spent rid-ing with her friends. However, her good mood started to fade slightly as she thought about the upcoming sleep-over. It really didn't promise to be much fun at all, between Mrs. Atwood's hovering and Tessa's very pres-ence. She wished again that they could have it in the loft instead. Maybe if they asked Max really, really nicely . . .

"Hello, Stevie." Mrs. Atwood's voice broke into her thoughts.

Stevie looked up in surprise. She was crossing the open area between the stable aisles and the tack room. Lisa's mother was heading toward her from the direction of the main entrance. "Oh!" Stevie said, her heart sinking. It looked as though they weren't even going to have another hour of peace. "Hi, Mrs. Atwood. Did you come to pick us up? That was nice of you. We should be ready soon."

Mrs. Atwood smiled. "I'm not here to pick you up," she replied with a rather odd smile. Stevie thought it might even be her version of a *mysterious* smile. That was strange. If there was one word that normally wouldn't be used to describe Lisa's mother, it was *mysterious*. "But I need your help for a moment. Could you get Lisa and Carole and meet me outside?"

Stevie shrugged. "Sure, I guess so," she mumbled, feeling confused. She tossed the bucket into the student locker room, where no horse could accidentally step in it, and hurried back toward Derby's stall.

Moments later all three girls were leaving the stable building and heading toward the Atwoods' car. Mrs. Atwood was standing near the open trunk, waiting for them.

"All right," she said briskly when the girls reached her. "Here are your things." She waved a hand at the trunk, which was stuffed full of suitcases, sleeping bags, and pillows. Lisa recognized her own things and Tessa's, as well as Stevie's and Lisa's, which their parents had dropped off at her house that morning.

Lisa stared at her mother, completely mystified. "What?" she said. "What's going on? Why did you bring this stuff here?"

Mrs. Atwood laughed. "Surprise!" she cried. "You're having your sleepover here—in the hayloft."

"But Max—" Carole blurted out, her brown eyes wide with confusion.

"It's all arranged," Mrs. Atwood said, her eyes twinkling. "Max gave his permission. It was all Tessa's idea."

"Tessa?" Stevie sounded stunned. "What are you talking about?"

Mrs. Atwood shrugged. "For some reason, Tessa really wanted your sleepover party to be in the hayloft." She wrinkled her nose in distaste. "I can't imagine why—it must be terribly dusty and hot up there. But I suppose it will be a novelty for her. She even promised to bring you all dinner."

Lisa wasn't really listening to her mother. She was trying to figure this out. "So Tessa decided we should have the sleepover at Pine Hollow," she murmured. "And she arranged it with you and Max."

Her mother gave her a perplexed look. "Of course, dear," she said. "Isn't that what I've just been saying?"

"I STILL CAN'T believe she came up with the same idea we did," Lisa said. It was a few minutes later. The girls' things were safely stowed in a corner of the big hayloft. Now Carole and Stevie were watching Lisa finish grooming Derby.

Carole nodded. She felt more confused than ever. "I

guess this goes to show that we're not on *totally* different wavelengths," she suggested.

"I don't know about that," Stevie said. She had gone to retrieve and fill Derby's water bucket. Now she hooked it in place. "She probably has some other motive in mind. Maybe she wants to ignore us as much as we want to ignore her." Her expression brightened at that thought.

Lisa sighed. "Well, I guess with Mom out of the picture, this sleepover might not be quite as bad," she muttered.

Carole was beginning to wonder if that was true. At least with Mrs. Atwood hanging around, the girls would have had to be polite to each other. With the way Stevie and Lisa were feeling about Tessa, Carole feared the worst. *Especially since I'm not exactly in the mood to play peacemaker*, she thought, remembering the water bucket incident. She bit her lip anxiously. No, she wasn't looking forward to this sleepover at all.

STEVIE, CAROLE, AND Lisa managed to keep themselves busy for the next few hours. They mucked out stalls. They swept the stable aisles. They knocked cobwebs out of the corners. They caught and led in horses that had spent the day in the paddocks and fields. Even after Tessa arrived, they hardly had time to say two words to her.

But after they finished helping Red with the evening feeding, there wasn't much left to do. Finally the girls had no choice. It was time for the sleepover to start.

Lisa reluctantly led the way as they climbed the wooden ladder to the loft. Tessa was already there. She had arranged their sleeping bags in a circle near the window and was busy unwrapping cold cuts and cheese on a picnic cloth on the loft floor. Other sandwich ingredients were ready nearby, along with bags of chips and popcorn. Several cans of soda and juice waited in a bucket of ice.

Lisa's stomach grumbled, and she realized she was famished. She was impressed that Tessa had laid out such a nice picnic. But she wasn't about to admit it. "Oh," she said with a bored shrug. "Is it time to eat already?"

Tessa smiled tentatively. "I hope it's okay," she said. "I picked up most of the food at the mall, and I wasn't sure what you'd like."

Stevie shrugged, too. "I guess it will do," she replied. "If I'm hungry enough, I can choke down almost anything."

Tessa's face fell. Carole, watching, felt a pang of guilt. This was all wrong. They shouldn't be acting so cold and mean. Tessa was their friend! Wasn't she? A vision of Tessa and Phil giggling together in the hallway outside the tack room floated into her mind. It was followed by the image of Lisa bent over a computer keyboard as the clock ticked toward midnight and Tessa slumbered in her cozy bed. And worst of all, there was the picture of Topside stepping into that metal bucket and pitching forward, his leg crumpling beneath him. . . .

Carole shook her head. It was all too much. "Okay, let's eat," she said in a brisk, businesslike tone. She sat

124

down across from Tessa and began assembling a sandwich without looking up.

Stevie and Lisa sat down on either side of her, forming a line facing Tessa, who sat alone on the other side of the food. None of them looked at her. None of them spoke.

Lisa was suddenly finding it difficult to keep the tears back. Her logical mind told her she was being silly. Tessa had proved herself unworthy of membership in The Saddle Club. She had betrayed Stevie by flirting with Phil. She had caused tons of extra work for Lisa and her mother without so much as offering to help. She had endangered Topside with her sloppy care. And to top it off, she had cast her friends aside in favor of their greatest enemy, Veronica diAngelo.

Her logical mind knew all that. But somehow her heart hadn't received the message. It still ached for the friendship she'd thought they had with Tessa. Lisa had to keep her eyes trained on her sandwich and blink rapidly to keep them from spilling over.

"So," Tessa said. Her voice was as bright and cheerful as ever, though Stevie thought she detected a slight quaver. "Did you all have a good day today?"

As Carole murmured a vague affirmative answer, Stevie gritted her teeth. She knew the best thing to do would be to keep silent. The sooner Tessa realized they weren't interested in small talk, the better. Then they could finish their dinner quickly and change into their pajamas. The earlier they all went to sleep, the earlier they could wake up—and the earlier this miserable sleepover would be over.

But Stevie had never been very good at keeping quiet. And she was even worse at keeping her feelings to herself. Why should she spare Tessa's feelings, anyway? Tessa was the one who was in the wrong. She was the one who had cast her eye on Stevie's boyfriend. She was the one who had caused problems everywhere she turned, whether it was with the point-to-point plans or at the stable. "We had a great day," she blurted out angrily. "At least until *you* got here."

Tessa's eyes widened in shock. Her cheeks flushed a mottled pink.

Carole and Lisa gasped, but neither of them said a thing.

"Oh," Tessa said in a small voice. "I see."

"And that's not all." Now that Stevie had started, she couldn't stop. "If you think Phil likes you, even a little bit, you're sadly mistaken. He would never fall for your pathetic flirting. And in case you haven't figured it out, we don't appreciate you inviting Veronica to our sleepover. And furthermore—"

"Wait." This time Tessa's voice was loud and firm. Even Stevie was startled into silence. "I think we have a problem here."

The comment was so ridiculously inadequate that Lisa almost laughed. "No kidding," she said instead. "But it's not *we* that have the problem. It's *you*." She knew that didn't make much sense, but Tessa seemed to understand perfectly.

"Just let me explain," she said. "We seem to have a few large misunderstandings."

Stevie and Lisa both looked stubborn, but Carole finally met Tessa's gaze. "All right," she answered for all three of them. "If you think you have something to tell us, you'd better go ahead."

Tessa took a deep breath. "All right, then," she said. "First of all, I want to apologize. I'm afraid I've been a bit daft—I just didn't see until now how much my behavior has been upsetting you."

Stevie's eyes widened in indignation. "What?" she sputtered. "How could you not realize it? You *knew* that Phil and I—"

"Wait," Tessa said again. "That's the first thing I want to clear up. I have no interest in Phil—except as a friend. I just needed him to help me with my plan."

"Your plan?" Lisa repeated, sounding confused.

Tessa nodded. "That's what this has all been about," she said, her words coming in a rush. "Plotting with Phil, befriending Veronica, gaining her trust . . ."

"Wait a minute." Understanding was dawning on Stevie's face. "Back up a second here. Don't you really like Veronica?"

Tessa laughed. "Don't be ridiculous!" she exclaimed,

sounding more like the Tessa they knew and loved than she had all week. "Who could possibly *like* that insufferable girl?"

"But—But *why?*" Carole still felt bewildered by all this—she was starting to realize that something very strange was going on. Something strange and, perhaps, not altogether terrible. "What's your big plan?"

Tessa shook her head reluctantly. "I can't tell you that," she replied. "I'm sorry, but it would ruin everything. The whole point of this was to make sure Max couldn't possibly fault you for what's going to happen." She sighed. "Although I'm beginning to suspect I went a bit too far in making sure you didn't know what was going on. I thought I was dropping a few hints here and there, but maybe they were too subtle."

"I guess they were," Lisa replied. Like her friends, she was realizing that they might have jumped to some incorrect conclusions in the past week—especially the one about Phil. After all, plotting against Veronica sounded a lot more in character for him than flirting with one of Stevie's best friends. But Lisa still had some questions that Tessa hadn't cleared up yet. "What about all that extra work you've been causing me and my mom with all your bright ideas about the point-to-point? Are you telling me you didn't realize you were doing that, either?"

Tessa gave her an apologetic look. "I realize my suggestion about the scurry race was rather impulsive," she admitted. The corners of her mouth turned up slightly. "Although actually it ended up working out perfectly."

"Not for me," Lisa replied. "I spent that entire afternoon as Mom's personal secretary."

"I'm really sorry about that." Tessa's forehead wrinkled with concern. "I meant to help out, I really did." She sighed. "But Veronica was *so* insistent that we go over to the Penningtons' that very day, even when I told her I thought I should go straight home with you to help out. And then once we were there she kept running off to make Miles show her this or that. I think she's really smitten with him."

"Hmmm," Stevie said. "I wonder."

Lisa gave her a surprised look. "Huh?" she said. "You mean about Veronica's crush on Miles? I thought that was obvious to everyone."

"Oh, it is," Stevie assured her. "No, I was just thinking about something else. Go on, Tessa."

Tessa shrugged. "I was finished."

"No, you weren't," Lisa insisted. "What about the other stuff? Like deciding to move the scurry race to the end of the schedule after the program was at the printer's?"

Tessa looked confused. "What does that have to do with me?" she said. "I thought Max decided that. That's what Veronica told me, anyway."

"But Veronica told *me* . . ." Lisa's voice trailed off.

She glanced at Stevie, who was looking more and more thoughtful by the second. "Oh," she said. "I see."

Carole still looked troubled. "There's something else," she said. "We've been covering for you so far. But I really thought you would take better care of Topside. No matter how distracted you were with your plotting and every-thing, there's no excuse for carelessness in the stable."

This time Tessa looked downright insulted. "What do you mean?" she protested. "I would never neglect a horse. I've taken perfect care of Topside ever since I got here!"

"Do you call leaving a metal water bucket sitting around his stall perfect care?" Carole shot back. "Plus, Max hates it when we go riding and leave the stall a mess. We told you that."

Lisa nodded. "And maybe being careless with tack isn't quite as bad as being careless with the horses themselves," she said, "but it took Carole ages to clean up after you in the tack room that time."

Tessa waved her hands wildly. "Hold on here!" she cried. "Have I been riding at a different stable all week? I don't know what you mean by any of this."

"I do." Stevie spoke so suddenly that all three of her friends turned to stare at her. She was smiling, but it wasn't a happy smile. It was the smile of someone who had finally figured out exactly what was going on. "We've been idiots," she said matter-of-factly.

"Huh?" Carole said.

Stevie shrugged. "Don't you see? We've missed a really

obvious point here. Namely, that there's no way that Veronica would ever want to be friends with Tessa."

"Hey," Tessa protested. "That's not very nice."

"No, listen," Stevie insisted. "Veronica hated you last week—because you're friends with us, because of what happened in England, and, well, just because you're a nice person instead of a shallow snake in the grass like her. And then you helped us humiliate her yet again—you can bet she knew that, even if Max didn't." She shrugged. "And suddenly, after that, she wants to kiss and make up? I don't think so."

Now that Lisa thought about it, it really didn't make much sense. She couldn't believe she'd missed it before. "Wait," she said. "But that means—"

"That Veronica was using Tessa for her own sneaky reasons," Stevie finished for her with a nod. "And I think it's obvious now what she was doing. Just think about it. Veronica invited Phil to the tack room with them. Then she left him alone with Tessa—with the door shut—and started talking about them in Danny's stall, where she knew we'd probably overhear."

Carole gasped. "That's true!" she said. "If we hadn't heard Veronica saying how she thought Tessa liked Phil, that never would have occurred to us."

"Actually, I was the one who shut the door, not Veronica," Tessa admitted. "And I may have given her the idea about liking Phil because I kept hinting for her to leave us alone. But it was only because I didn't want her to hear me talking about her. I never imagined she'd turn it into that sort of gossip."

Stevie nodded sympathetically. "That's Veronica for you," she said. "She found a surefire way to get me mad at Tessa. Then there was Lisa."

"Right," Lisa said. It was all becoming clearer by the second. "When she found out Tessa and I were going to the mall with Mom, she made sure to turn up and drag Tessa away." She smiled ruefully. "I guess even Veronica realizes that shopping with my mom isn't the highlight of my day."

"Then she must have come up with the idea to switch the order of the program," Tessa said, catching on. "She told me it was Max's idea, but she told you it was mine, so you'd think I was the one causing you and your mum all sorts of work."

Carole thought all of that was very interesting. But she was still thinking about Topside. "But what about that metal bucket?" she said. "And the dirty stall we cleaned up for you?"

"I never knew a thing about either," Tessa told her. "I never used anything but Topside's regular plastic bucket. And I *always* attached it to the hook."

"Veronica again," Stevie said with grim satisfaction. "She's the only person I know who would endanger a horse like that and not even think about it, except as a means to her own ends."

Lisa shook her head. "Actually, I'm a little shocked," she admitted. "That's nasty, even for her."

Tessa was looking thoughtful. "Which day did you find the stall dirty?" she asked.

"Um . . . It was Wednesday, I think," Lisa said, thinking back. "When you and Veronica were out on that long trail ride."

Tessa nodded. "Just as I thought," she said. "That was the day Veronica suddenly remembered she had to call home. We were halfway across the first pasture, but she insisted she would just be a few minutes." She laughed ruefully. "I must have ridden Topside around that pasture fifty times while I was waiting for her to get back. But I never thought twice about it."

"Veronica can be pretty sneaky," Stevie agreed. "She must have run back and carted some old manure into the stall from the muck heap." She glanced at Carole. "Which explains why you thought it looked funny. I'll bet she was the one who knocked down all that tack in the tack room after Tessa and Phil left. She probably snuck in while we were checking our horses and quietly made a mess. And I'm sure she planted that icky sandwich by her new boots, too, just hoping I'd do something about it and she could tattle to Max."

"So Veronica was trying to mess up our friendship with Tessa all along." Carole finally understood.

"And it almost worked." Lisa scooted around the picnic cloth until she was sitting next to Tessa. Then she smiled tentatively. "Can you forgive us?" she asked.

Tessa nodded immediately. "Absolutely," she assured all of them. "And can you all forgive me for being so thickheaded? I still can't believe it reached this point before I noticed. I guess I was too caught up in my own plans to pay enough attention to you."

"It happens," Stevie said sympathetically. "Believe me, I know. Anyway, it's partly our fault, too. We should have trusted you more."

"And even if we had doubts, we should have talked to you about them," Carole put in. She scooted around until she was sitting on Tessa's other side, and gave her a hug. "But don't worry. No matter who should have done what, the important thing is that we're all still friends."

"We are, aren't we?" Tessa asked, still looking a little worried.

This time all three original members of The Saddle Club grabbed her in a big group hug. "Absolutely," they said in one voice.

Soon they were all hungrily chewing their sandwiches, washing them down with the drinks Tessa had brought. "This is great," Carole said, her mouth full of potato chips.

Stevie was eating just as enthusiastically as the others. But she was thinking about something at the same time. "So, Tessa," she said, a bit too casually. "About this plan of yours . . ."

Tessa held up one hand warningly. "Sorry, Stevie," she said with a grin. "I already told you. I really can't give you any details about that. I have to protect your—your—" She searched for the words.

"Plausible deniability?" Lisa offered helpfully, reaching for another slice of cheese.

Tessa nodded. "That's it," she said. "If you don't know anything, you can't be blamed."

Carole and Lisa nodded agreeably, but Stevie still wasn't satisfied. "But Tessa . . . ," she began in a whine.

"Stevie, really!" Tessa cut her off. "Please let it drop. I assure you, all will become clear tomorrow. Even after all this, don't you trust me?"

Stevie sighed with frustration. "That's not the problem," she said. "I'll trust you till the cows come home. I'm just afraid I'll die of curiosity way before then!"

11

DESPITE HER DIRE prediction, Stevie managed to survive the sleepover. And soon after the morning of the point-to-point dawned, she was too busy to spare a thought for Tessa's scheme.

Max put The Saddle Club to work as soon as the four girls clambered down from the loft, yawning and rubbing their eyes. There were horses to be fed and groomed, stalls to be cleaned, horse trailers to be readied, tack to check, traveling bandages to put on . . . the list went on and on. Luckily Tessa had remembered to have Mrs. Atwood pack the clothes Lisa and she would be wearing to the event, along with everything Stevie and Carole had brought to Lisa's. They washed up and changed in the stable's bathroom moments before it was time to load the horses that would be competing in the event into Pine Hollow's trailers.

Soon a caravan of horse trailers was trundling through Willow Creek on the way to the country club on the other side of town. Carole and Stevie were crowded into the cab of the one being driven by Red O'Malley. Starlight and Belle were in the back, along with a couple of horses belonging to Max's adult riders.

"This is exciting, isn't it?" Carole said happily.

Stevie nodded. "Maybe even more exciting than we think," she said. "I wonder what Tessa is—"

Carole elbowed her before she could say anything about Tessa's plan. She glanced at Red worriedly. But the stable hand didn't seem to have heard a word. He had just steered his vehicle over a slight rise in the road, and the grounds of the Willow Creek Country Club were spread out before them. "Wow," he commented with a low whistle. "Those country club folks really went all out for this."

The girls saw what he meant. It really was amazing. The broad, sweeping fields that flanked the golf course had been transformed into a sort of fairgrounds, with large, colorful tents dotting the landscape. The girls could also see where several courses had been marked off for the races, with broad timber fences all along them. Temporary grandstand seating had been set up near the finish line of each course.

"Amazing," Carole said breathlessly. Her heart started to beat a little faster with excitement. She couldn't wait for the point-to-point to start!

The girls helped unload the horses and make them comfortable in the large tents serving as temporary stables. Then, with Max's permission, they hurried off to check out the scene.

Visitors were already pouring in through the front gates. People of all ages crowded into the refreshment and craft booths, wandered over to look at the course, found seats in the stands, or set up tailgate picnics in the parking lot. Lively music played over the public-address system, mostly patriotic marches in honor of July Fourth, which was the following day. Volunteers scurried around, answering questions, picking up trash, and generally being helpful. Lisa spotted her mother behind the counter at one of the craft booths, helping an elderly woman choose a T-shirt for her small granddaughter.

"It looks like the fund-raiser is going to be a big success," Carole remarked as the girls strolled past the ticket table, where half a dozen volunteers struggled to tear tickets and make change fast enough to keep up with the demand.

"Cool," Stevie said with a smile. "That means they'll probably want to do this every year!"

"I hope so." Lisa glanced at a nearby refreshment tent. "Hey, is it just me or did we forget to eat breakfast? I'm starving!"

138

"Me too," Stevie said. "Come on, let's go rustle up some grub. We've got to keep our energy up for the race later on."

Tessa glanced at her watch. "Count me out," she said reluctantly. "I'll grab something later. I'm supposed to be at the main stage in exactly three minutes."

"You are?" Carole looked surprised. "What for?"

Tessa just winked in reply. "See you in a little while." With that, she disappeared into the crowds.

Her friends had just settled down at an empty picnic table when the sprightly strains of "Liberty Bell March" were cut off abruptly. After a moment of static, the PA system crackled to life again.

"Good morning, ladies and gentlemen," said a very familiar voice. "It's my pleasure to welcome you to the first annual Willow Creek Point-to-Point."

Carole, Stevie, and Lisa exchanged glances. "Tessa!" they cried in one voice. They grabbed their food and hurried out of the refreshment tent. Sure enough, once they were outside they could see their friend standing on the temporary stage near the finish line of the main racecourse. She was standing between Mrs. diAngelo and an older woman, whom Lisa recognized as the president of the country club.

"I do hope you're all enjoying the hospitality," Tessa went on. "I want to thank some of our generous sponsors . . ."

"I thought Veronica was supposed to make the opening

remarks today," Lisa commented as Tessa went on to list the names of the local businesses that had donated food and other supplies. "She's been bragging about it for weeks."

Stevie grinned. "I guess this is what Tessa was talking about," she said admiringly. "Pretty good plan. Veronica must be fuming."

Just then Carole spotted a familiar figure standing to one side of the stage. It was Veronica, and she didn't look happy. In fact, she was scowling darkly at Tessa, her arms folded over her chest. "Definitely," Carole agreed, pointing. "But why do you think Tessa was so worried about us finding out? There's no way Veronica could pin this on us—not if her own mother agreed to let Tessa speak."

Lisa shrugged. "Maybe she just didn't want to take any chances."

The girls listened as Tessa completed her opening remarks. When she stepped away from the microphone, they applauded enthusiastically. They applauded just as enthusiastically when they saw Max climbing onto the stage. He took the microphone and gave a brief talk explaining the history and purpose of point-to-point racing and outlining the rules and entry requirements for each of the day's events, including the junior hurdle, which was open only to riders under the age of sixteen, and the scurry race.

"There are no cash prizes for the winners of today's

races," Max said in conclusion. "Just ribbons and the fun of competing. So let's go out there and have fun!"

A cheer went up from the crowd, and the point-to-point began in earnest.

A few minutes later Tessa found her friends in the crowd lined up along the course for the first race, which was due to start soon. "Hi!" she said breathlessly. "How was I?"

"Fantastic," Carole declared, giving her a quick hug. "We were so surprised!"

"Thanks," Tessa said. "Oh, and there's more good news. You don't have to feel sorry for me anymore about not riding in the junior hurdle. I may just have a chance for a ribbon today after all."

"Really? How?" Lisa asked.

"Mrs. Pennington invited me to ride with her in the scurry race," Tessa replied happily. She shot them an anxious look. "You don't mind, do you? It will mean I can't ride with you in the pony cart . . ."

"Don't worry about it," Carole assured her. "You can't pass up this chance. This way you'll probably be able to put Veronica in her place again—Mrs. Pennington is sure to take the blue ribbon, so Veronica and Miles will just have to settle for second best."

"If they're lucky," Lisa joked. "Knowing Veronica, she'll probably make Miles drive slowly so that her hair won't get messed up."

Stevie laughed. "It serves her right that she didn't get to make that speech," she said. She grinned at Tessa admiringly. "What a terrific prank. How did you do it?"

"It was a piece of cake," Tessa said. "Mrs. diAngelo absolutely insisted I speak."

"Well, Veronica must be furious," Carole said. "She told half the county she was going to be the opening speaker today."

"I suppose she is a bit miffed at me right now." Tessa shrugged and winked. "But that's nothing to how angry she'll be a bit later."

Stevie's eyes widened. "You mean there's more?"

Tessa just grinned and winked again. "Come on," she said. "Let's watch the race." And that was all she would say.

For The Saddle Club, the next few hours seemed to pass in the blink of an eye. Before they knew it, they were saddling up their horses for the junior hurdle race.

"Good luck," Tessa said as she gave Carole a leg up. "I'll be rooting for you."

"Thanks," said Carole, Lisa, and Stevie in one voice. They knew Tessa's luck was meant for all of them.

Max hustled by at that moment. When he saw Tessa standing there, he pointed at her. "Tessa," he barked. "They're looking for you at the judging stand. Move it!"

"Now I really feel like part of the Pine Hollow crew," Tessa whispered with a giggle before scurrying off.

The others rode their horses into an open area behind the stabling tent to warm them up. Lisa paid close attention as she guided Derby around in a broad circle at a smooth canter, asking him to lengthen his strides, then to switch leads. The big, athletic horse obeyed every order instantly and eagerly, and Lisa smiled. She was ready.

Soon it was time to head to the starting line. Unlike flat racing, in which the horses break out of a starting gate, in this type of racing they simply formed a more or less straight line across the track.

Lisa moved Derby forward a few steps until she was even with Stevie and Belle on one side and a girl she recognized as a member of Cross County's Pony Club on the other. Glancing down the line on either side of her, she saw Carole, Phil, Phil's friend A.J., Veronica, and several other Pine Hollow riders. All of them looked eager to compete.

Max was acting as the starter for the race. He stepped forward, and Lisa stopped paying attention to everything else. Now only she and Derby mattered. She leaned forward a little and waited for Max to give the signal. There was a tense moment of silence.

"Go!" Max shouted at last, dropping his arm.

The horses surged forward. Lisa gave Derby the signal to gallop, but she held him in check for the first few strides. She didn't want him to stumble or lose his balance, and there would be plenty of time to fight for the lead later. All around her, Lisa heard the other riders calling encouragement to their mounts. She was aware of the racers on either side, some leaping forward, some hanging back. But she kept her eyes trained on her own horse and the course before them as she waited for Derby to find his stride.

The big gelding was confident and surefooted, and soon he was galloping strongly, his ears pitched forward. They were approaching the first jump.

Like the other riders, Lisa had walked the course earlier in the day. She had also led Derby over to give him a look at the fences. Now all Lisa had to do was guide the two of them safely over the dozen obstacles standing between them and the finish line.

She shortened her reins slightly to steady the horse, quickly judging the distance remaining to the fence. Four strides, three strides, two . . . On the last stride, Derby gathered himself for takeoff. He soared forward and up, leaving the ground perfectly with inches to spare between his front hooves and the top rail. For a second, Lisa was distracted by the sensation of many horses jumping the long fence on either side of her. But she snapped back to attention in time to adjust her position as Derby hit the ground running on the far side.

"Way to go, boy!" she shouted into the wind as the horse hurtled forward toward the next jump.

Out of the corner of her eye, Lisa saw Tessa studying the horses going over the fifth jump. Lisa admired the way

Tessa concentrated on her own attention on the task, and it made Lisa focus her

By the seventh fence, Lisa had settled into the rhythm of the race well enough to start thinking about their position. There were several horses ahead of her, and she noted that Carole and Veronica were among them. Even over the noise of the thundering hooves and the cheering crowd, she could hear Stevie behind her, shouting encouragement to Belle.

Lisa hunched down a little lower over Derby's neck. "Come on, boy," she whispered. She knew he couldn't possibly hear her, but she was sure that somehow he knew what she wanted him to do. "Let's show them what you're made of." She urged him on even faster with all her aids, and the horse responded. At the next fence, he was even with Veronica and Danny. Starlight was only a few strides ahead.

After that, the five leaders switched positions from stride to stride. Lisa continued to talk softly to Derby as he ran with all his might. As they cleared the final fence, she let out a whoop. "Come on, Derby!" she shrieked. _"Go for it!"_

The big horse found the energy to surge forward even faster. But the other racers were running their hearts out, too. As the finish line flashed by, Lisa could see that Carole had won. But she also knew that she had come in second.

"Yeee-ha!" she cried ha... She pulled Derby back to
a canter, then a trot... a was a perfectionist, which
meant she often was... content unless she was first. But in
this case, she w... thrilled with second place. Her new
partnership w... Derby had worked out better than she
could eve... have hoped. She patted the horse fondly on
his sweaty shoulder. "You were amazing, boy," she told
him. "If Prancer were here, even *she* would be impressed!"

"I STILL CAN'T BELIEVE Veronica beat me," Stevie groaned
for about the fourteenth time. The junior hurdle had
ended a little more than an hour before, and The Saddle
Club, including Phil and A.J. but minus Tessa, was sitting
in the grandstand waiting for the start of the scurry race,
the final event of the day.

Phil rolled his eyes. "You know she must be upset about
this," he commented to Carole and Lisa with a grin.
"She's hardly said a word about beating *me*."

Carole laughed. Veronica had placed third in the race,
just half a step ahead of fourth-place finishers Stevie and
Belle. Phil had come in sixth. "Just enjoy it," she advised
Phil. "I'm sure she'll get around to teasing you sooner or
later."

"Probably sooner," Phil agreed, and Stevie shot him a
dirty look.

Carole leaned back against the bleacher seat behind
her. "By the way, Phil," she said. "We know you've been
sworn to secrecy. But when exactly are we going to find

out the details of this grand scheme you and Tessa have cooked up?" Except for the opening speech, the day had passed without incident in regard to Veronica. The girls were still waiting to find out what else their friend had planned.

Phil shrugged and looked mysterious. "Don't worry," he said. "It won't be long now. Not long at all."

Just then Mrs. diAngelo's voice blared out over the PA system, announcing that the scurry race was about to begin.

Carole sat forward eagerly, all thoughts of Veronica instantly banished from her mind. She couldn't wait. She had been looking forward to the scurry race almost as much as she'd been looking forward to the junior hurdle. A course marked by cones and balls was already laid out for the event. A large digital clock, easily visible to the spectators, was ready to tick off the seconds it took each carriage team to complete the twisting, turning course. Mrs. diAngelo would announce the final time and faults for each team, as well as keeping the audience apprised of the standings.

"Here we go," Stevie said as the first team entered the makeshift show ring. It was Mr. Baker from Cross County, driving a fancy-looking carriage behind a pair of palominos.

"Yo, Mr. Baker!" Phil shouted over the noise of the crowd as his riding instructor took a warm-up lap around the ring.

A.J. added a whoop of his own. "Looking good!" he cried.

Mr. Baker didn't respond, but his wife, seated beside him, glanced up at Phil and A.J. and gave them a thumbs-up.

Mr. Baker turned in a respectable performance, knocking down only one ball and finishing well within the time allowed. He kept the palominos to a steady, fast trot, speeding up to a canter only on one long straightaway in the middle of the course and the brief distance between the final pair of cones and the finish line. The Saddle Club cheered lustily as Mrs. diAngelo announced the time and faults.

"This is fun already," Lisa said.

"You ain't seen nothing yet," Carole promised. "It gets more and more exciting as the teams try to beat each other's scores."

She was right. The next team, sponsored by the local fire department, was a pair of huge dappled grays pulling an antique fire wagon. The wagon and the horses appeared impossibly large for the tight turns on the course, but that didn't stop them from equaling Mr. Baker's faults and beating his time by almost two full seconds.

"Wow," Lisa said, impressed, as the team trotted out of the ring to enthusiastic applause. "They were good. Did you see the way they cantered around those turns?"

A.J. nodded. "Check it out," he said. "Here comes team number three." He pointed to a pair of tall, elegant black warmbloods driven by a distinguished-looking man in white tie and tails.

Carole stood up. "Come on, you guys," she said reluctantly to Stevie and Lisa. "We'd better go bring out the ponies. We're supposed to be number nine." Red had promised to harness the ponies for them, but the girls wanted to be there in plenty of time to help. They said good-bye to the two boys, who weren't competing in the scurry race, and hurried back to the harnessing area.

When they got there, Veronica was one of the first people they saw. She spotted them immediately and rushed over with a frown. "Have any of you seen Miles?" she snapped. "We're supposed to go on in a few minutes, and I haven't seen him in hours. He was supposed to meet me here with my costume." She smiled at that thought. "I can't wait to see what it looks like. He promised me it would be fabulous."

Stevie was staring over her shoulder. She had just spotted a team approaching. It was too far away for her to see the driver's face, but she had the funniest feeling she already knew who it was. "Um, is that him coming now?" she asked casually, pointing.

Veronica whirled around, looking relieved. But her expression soon changed to one of confusion, followed by disbelief. Finally it transformed again into a glare of pure rage.

It *was* Miles Pennington driving toward them. His team was moving briskly and smoothly, and his vehicle was obviously in perfect condition. But the whole picture in no way resembled the dignified splendor of his grandmother's team.

"Are those—" Lisa began slowly, hardly believing her eyes.

Carole nodded, her own gaze trained on the approaching pair. "Mules," she finished with a nod.

The large beasts pulling the cart were indeed mules. *Big* mules. They each stood around sixteen hands high, with shaggy dark coats, gray muzzles, and enormous tufted ears that swiveled alertly as they trotted along in perfect harmony. They couldn't have looked more different from Mrs. Pennington's sleek, smooth Cleveland Bays. But the contrast between the mules' cart and Mrs. Pennington's elegant phaeton was even greater. Miles was seated on the high front seat of a humble wooden farm wagon. Bales of hay weighted down the long, slatted back, and painted on the sides were the words: HAYRIDES, 5¢. Miles himself was dressed in a red-and-white-checked shirt, faded denim overalls, and a ragged straw hat. To complete the look, a long piece of straw was clenched between his teeth, which were all showing in a broad grin.

"Howdy, everyone!" he cried playfully as he pulled his team to a halt in front of them. "Howdy, Miss Veronica. I've got your costume here." He tossed her a bundle of clothes that had been sitting on the seat beside him.

Veronica jumped back as if she feared the clothes would burn her. The bundle fell to the ground, and The

Saddle Club could see that the outfit exactly matched what Miles was wearing.

Stevie was grinning so hard she feared her face would crack in two. So *this* was Tessa's master plan! She waited to see what would happen next.

What happened next was that Veronica threw a tantrum. "I thought you said your team was a pair of valuable horses from France!" she shouted at Miles, stamping her foot angrily. She seemed to have forgotten all about The Saddle Club.

Miles shrugged. "Well, that's two-thirds right." He waved a hand at the mules, who were flicking their long ears curiously at the girls. "These guys are Poitevin mules, which are the offspring of a breed of workhorse called the Poitevin and a type of jackass known as Baudet de Poitou, both of which come from the Poitou region in western France. They're really quite unusual, especially in this country. But you must have misheard me on the horse part. As you can see, they're mules, and proud of it."

Veronica glared at him, her face bright red. "You must think this is some kind of a joke," she huffed. "Well, the joke's on you. There's no way I'm riding in that ridiculous cart. And I'm certainly not putting on these hideous clothes." She kicked the costume.

Max walked by just in time to overhear. As soon as she spotted him, Stevie nudged her friends. They fell back slightly, hoping he wouldn't notice them watching. "Is there a problem here?" he asked Veronica.

Veronica tipped her nose into the air. "See for yourself," she sniffed haughtily. "Can you believe Miles actually expected me to ride in that thing with him?"

Max raised one eyebrow. "I don't know what Miles may be expecting," he said evenly. "But I'll tell you what I'm expecting, and that's for you to ride as part of this team as you promised, unless you have an awfully good excuse."

Veronica grabbed the denim overalls off the dusty ground. When she held them up, The Saddle Club could see that one knee was patched with a large appliqué sunflower. "What more excuse do I need than this?" she cried. "I wouldn't be caught dead in this horrible outfit."

Max glanced at his watch. "Enough, Veronica," he snapped. "I have things to do. Now put on those clothes and get in that cart—*if* you want to ride at my stable again anytime before Christmas, that is."

Veronica just goggled at him for a second. "You can't be serious," she said at last.

Max didn't reply. He just gave her a stern look and marched off.

For a moment Veronica seemed about to rush after him. Then her shoulders slumped. She stared blankly at the overalls in her hand.

"Hurry up, Ronnie," Miles called cheerfully. "We don't want to hold things up."

The Saddle Club had to rush to get ready for their turn in the ring, so they didn't get to actually watch Veronica pull her costume over her regular riding clothes. But since

152

the mule team performed just before their pony team, they did get to witness her performance in the ring.

"Wow," Stevie said from her seat in the pony cart, which was waiting just beyond the gate. "I think her face is even redder than her shirt."

Carole grinned. "It looks like she refused her piece of straw," she pointed out. "Miles has two pieces sticking out of his mouth now."

"Is it my imagination, or is Veronica doing her best to keep her face turned away from the bleachers?" Lisa put in.

"I don't know about that," Carole replied. "But if she pulls that straw hat any lower over her forehead, she can start using the fringe for dental floss."

All the girls laughed. Despite their enjoyment of Veronica's predicament, they couldn't help noticing the expert way Miles drove his mule team through the course. He kept them at a steady canter through most of the twists and turns, slowing to a trot only in one or two particularly tricky spots, and breaking into a gallop on the straightaways. When he finished, he was in first place out of the teams that had competed so far.

"Wow," Carole said. "That was great. Maybe a blue ribbon will help Veronica get over her embarrassment."

"I certainly hope not," Stevie said. "It must have taken Tessa lots of effort to set this up. We don't want Veronica to end up being *happy* about the whole thing."

"I don't think you have to worry about that." Lisa was

still watching Veronica's face. As the crowd leaped to its feet to applaud the mule team's incredible finish, her cheeks turned from bright red to a deeper tone that could only be described as magenta. A photographer from the local newspaper leaped forward to snap a picture. Before Veronica could react, Miles grabbed her hand and raised their arms together in victory, grinning gleefully and tipping his straw hat to the camera. As the shutter clicked, Veronica's face was caught in a peevish scowl. Lisa laughed. "No, I think Veronica will remember this moment for a long, long time."

IN THE END, Veronica had to comfort herself with a red ribbon for second place. Mrs. Pennington had come in first with Hodge and Podge. The Saddle Club's pony cart finished a distant ninth, having knocked over three balls and barely beaten the maximum time. But the girls didn't mind one bit. The scurry race had been fun, and that was what counted. Well, that and the joy of seeing Veronica put in her place.

"So?" Tessa said expectantly with a grin, catching up to them after the ribbons had been handed out. "What d'you think?"

Stevie flung her arms around Tessa and spun her around in an enthusiastic embrace. "I think you're the most wonderful person who ever lived!" she cried.

Tessa flushed, laughing as she struggled to free herself. "Thanks, Stevie," she said, straightening the blue ribbon pinned to her jacket, which had been knocked askew by Stevie's hug.

"You really are amazing, you know," Lisa said, smiling at Tessa. "It would take a lot to make up for all the grief and misunderstandings of the past week. But this did it. It really did."

And not one member of The Saddle Club could disagree with that.

"So when do these fireworks start, anyway?" Tessa asked with a yawn.

It was the next day, July Fourth. Tessa, Lisa, Carole, and Stevie were stretched out on a picnic blanket on a hillside at the edge of the country club's golf course. They had spent the day at Willow Creek's annual parade, and now, as dusk fell, they were waiting for the fireworks display to begin.

"Be patient," Stevie told her. "It's better if it's completely dark before they start."

Tessa sat up and grinned at her. "Do my ears deceive me?" she joked. "Is this really Stevie Lake telling me to be patient? The girl who almost badgered me to death trying to find out my master plan?"

All the girls laughed at that. Lisa glanced over her shoulder at the field behind her. Most of the paraphernalia of the point-to-point had been disassembled, but the country club had left up several of the refreshment tents in anticipation of the crowds coming to watch the fireworks. Phil and A.J. had just departed in search of food and drinks for all of them. At the moment, Lisa could see that there were large crowds thronging around the tents. She guessed that the boys wouldn't be back anytime soon.

Carole was still lying flat on her back with her hands behind her head, gazing upward at the stars blinking on in the darkening sky. "Riding in the parade today was fun, wasn't it?" she mused. "I'm glad Miles asked us."

"Me too," Tessa said. "That was Miles's only condition to helping out with my plan—I had to agree that we'd all ride with him today." The girls, along with Phil and A.J., had all dressed up as scarecrows and ridden in the mule cart in the parade. "Though I'll never live it down back home if anyone finds out I actually helped to celebrate a war that England lost," she added with a laugh.

Stevie sat up, too. "Speaking of your plan," she said, "you still haven't given us all the details. How on earth did you work it all out?"

"It wasn't so hard, really, once I found out about the mules," Tessa said. "I'd been driving myself mad trying to figure out what to do. But when Mrs. Pennington told me about some of the elaborate costumes people sometimes wear in scurry races—"

"She must have told you this while Veronica was out of the room," Lisa guessed.

"Oh, yes," Tessa replied. "Veronica was off somewhere trying to make Miles fall in love with her." She grinned. "Of course, that made it all the more perfect. And when Mrs. Pennington mentioned the mules, well . . ."

Stevie nodded. "All the pieces fell into place." She sighed happily. "I love it when that happens. A perfectly planned scheme is like nothing else in the world."

"A fat lot you would know about that," Carole said, shooting Stevie a wry look. "Lately your schemes haven't exactly been perfect."

"Are you still thinking about that water balloon thing?" Stevie waved one hand airily. "Forget it, will you? After all, Max finally did." After the point-to-point the evening before, Max had pulled the girls aside long enough to tell them that their probation was officially over.

"That doesn't mean you can start goofing off again, of course," he had said, giving Stevie an especially meaningful look.

Stevie had smiled innocently. "Of course not, Max," she had replied. "We'll go right on being our usual serious selves."

Lisa smiled as she thought about the disgruntled look Max had given them before hurrying off. Then she turned to Tessa curiously. "There's one thing I've been meaning to ask you," she said. "How did you figure out that making

158

Veronica look like a fashion victim in front of an audience was the best way to get back at her? Was it all that time you spent with her at the mall?"

"Well, that too," Tessa said. "But mostly it was Phil's idea. That's why I wanted his help. I knew he knew her much better than I did." She grinned. "Phil even went over to Miles's place the other night to help put the costumes together."

Stevie nodded as yet another piece fell into place. "So that's who he was visiting in Willow Creek," she murmured.

Carole was thinking about something else. "So in a way, it really was a Saddle Club team effort," she pointed out. "Even though Stevie and Lisa and I had no idea what was going on."

Tessa grinned. "Righto," she affirmed. "Isn't that what The Saddle Club is all about?"

"Speaking of teamwork," Stevie said, "I think Max may have been on our team yesterday more than we realized."

"What do you mean?" Carole asked.

Stevie shrugged. "Well, first of all, there was the way he forced Veronica to ride in the wagon when she was going to refuse."

"That was the one thing I was worried about," Tessa admitted. "If Max hadn't come along, Miles was going to start acting all lovey-dovey and begging her to do it for his sake. But we weren't sure even Veronica's crush would carry us that far."

159

"It probably wouldn't have," Stevie said. "But thanks to Max, it didn't have to. Besides, I have the funniest feeling that wasn't the only favor he did us." She grinned. "After all, he was one of the judges for the whole day, right? Don't you think he might have had something to do with Veronica's winning that award for best dressed?"

The others laughed and agreed. At the end of the scurry race, there had been a brief awards ceremony. Ribbons had been handed out in a variety of categories—for the fastest and most beautiful horses, the most lavish tailgate picnic, the cutest baby in attendance, and all sorts of other things. Veronica—with Miles—had won the ribbon for best dressed, forcing her to go onstage in her overalls to accept the prize from the country club president. And once again, the newspaper photographer had been there to record it all.

"The only thing that would have made it a teeny bit better is if I could have arranged for her to get that hideous tie instead of her ribbon," Stevie said, referring to the prank that had started this whole thing back on the last day of school. "Maybe I'll mail it to her." She leaned back on the blanket again, a contented smile on her face. "Anyway," she went on lazily, "my point is, Max came through for us as usual."

The others thought about that for a second. "I guess you're right," Lisa said at last. "Does that mean he wasn't as mad at us as we thought?"

"Who knows?" Carole said. "Max can be hard to figure

out sometimes." She sighed. "I'm just glad we're not on probation anymore. What a relief!"

The others agreed wholeheartedly. "That was really the problem all along, wasn't it?" Tessa pointed out. "If you hadn't been, we could have fought back from the beginning." She shrugged. "I mean, you wouldn't believe how awful I felt when Veronica kept baiting me last week. Not just because of what she said and did, but because I knew it was driving you crazy on my behalf. And because I was afraid you'd end up getting your riding privileges suspended because of it."

"I know," Lisa said. "Was that really why you were nice to Veronica at first?"

"At first," Tessa confirmed, nodding. "When Veronica first started being nice to me last weekend, I just wanted to keep things calm. Then when she seemed so eager to be best buddies, and tried to come between the four of us, I realized that she was up to her old tricks. So then . . ."

"The rest was history," Carole finished with a grin. "I still can't believe Veronica didn't figure out what really happened."

Tessa shrugged. "It was a foolproof plan," she declared. "Miles took full public credit for inventing those costumes and springing them on Veronica like that. He was a real sport about the whole thing—actually, I think he enjoyed it just as much as we did. And I believe Veronica thinks she was responsible for wheedling her way into riding with him in the scurry race." She grinned. "And she and I were together so much this week that as far as she knows, there's no way I could have known about those mules any more than she did. Let alone any of you."

Stevie sighed. "That's really the only bad thing about all this," she mused. "Veronica will never know how brilliant The Saddle Club really is."

"Stevie . . . ," Lisa began.

Stevie grinned. "Don't worry. My lips are sealed." She shrugged. "Anyway, it worked out perfectly, like I said. Veronica's interest in Tessa stopped just as quickly as her crush on Miles did. So now we can all enjoy the last couple of days of Tessa's visit."

"I think what you're trying to say," Lisa said, leaning on her elbow to look at Stevie, "is 'All's well that ends well.' "

"Something like that." Stevie stretched her arms above her head and then turned to smile at Tessa. "I'm just sorry that you have to leave in two days."

"Me too," Tessa agreed. "But don't fret. That still gives us almost forty-eight more hours for visiting—"

"And riding," Carole put in quickly.

Lisa nodded. "And planning more visits."

"Right," Tessa said. "Next time, it's your turn to come back to England. But for now, we still have time for at least one more sleepover . . ."

"And more riding," Carole supplied with a laugh.

"And going to TD's," Stevie suggested.

"And talking," Lisa said.

"And watching fireworks!" a new voice put in.

The girls looked up. Phil had just returned with an armful of food. A.J. was right behind him with a cardboard carton filled with soda cups.

The girls glanced around. Sure enough, the sky was completely dark, except for the stars twinkling high above. "They'll be starting any second now," A.J. predicted.

The end of his sentence was almost drowned out—first by the patriotic music that started pouring out of the loudspeakers set up behind the field, and then by the booming sound of a Roman candle shooting high into the night sky. It exploded into shards of color, and almost before the watchers could gasp in amazement, a bright flower-shaped cloud of red, white, and blue sparks burst just above it.

"This is perfect," Tessa declared.

Her friends weren't exactly sure whether she was referring to the warm summer night, the old-fashioned, all-American excitement of the Fourth of July fireworks display, her visit to the United States, or simply The Saddle Club itself. But any way they looked at it, Carole, Stevie, and Lisa had to agree that their good friend Tessa was absolutely right.

What happens to The Saddle Club next?
Read Bonnie Bryant's exciting new series
and find out.

High school. Driver's licenses. Boyfriends. Jobs.

A lot of new things are happening, but one thing remains the same: Stevie Lake, Lisa Atwood, and Carole Hanson are still best friends. However, even among best friends some things do change, and problems can strain any friendship . . . but these three can handle it. Can't they?

Read an excerpt from Pine Hollow #1: *The Long Ride*.

PROLOGUE

"DO YOU THINK we'll get there in time?" Stevie Lake asked, looking around for some reassuring sign that the airport was near.

"Since that plane almost landed on us, I think it's safe to say that we're close," Carole Hanson said.

"Turn right here," said Callie Forester from the backseat.

"And then left up ahead," Carole advised, picking out directions from the signs that flashed past near the airport entrance. "I think Lisa's plane is leaving from that terminal there."

"Which one?"

"The one we just passed," Callie said.

"Oh," said Stevie. She gripped the steering wheel tightly and looked for a way to turn around without causing a major traffic tie-up.

"This would be easier if we were on horseback," said Carole.

"Everything's easier on horseback," Stevie agreed.

"Or if we had a police escort," said Callie.

"Have you done that?" Stevie asked, trying to maneuver the car across three lanes of traffic.

"I have," said Callie. "It's kind of fun, but dangerous. It makes you think you're almost as important as other people tell you you are."

Stevie rolled her window down and waved wildly at the confused drivers around her. Clearly, her waving confused them more, but it worked. All traffic stopped. She crossed the necessary three lanes and pulled onto the service road.

It took another ten minutes to get back to the right and then ten more to find a parking place. Five minutes into the terminal. And then all that was left was to find Lisa.

"Where do you think she is?" Carole asked.

"I know," said Stevie. "Follow me."

"That's what we've been doing all morning," Callie said dryly. "And look how far it's gotten us."

But she followed anyway.

ALEX LAKE REACHED across the table in the airport cafeteria and took Lisa Atwood's hand.

"It's going to be a long summer," he said.

Lisa nodded. Saying good-bye was one of her least favorite activities. She didn't want Alex to know how hard it was, though. That would just make it tougher on him. The two of them had known each other for four years—as long as Lisa had been best friends with Alex's twin sister, Stevie. But they'd only started dating six months earlier. Lisa could hardly believe that. It seemed as if she'd been in love with him forever.

"But it is just for the summer," she said. The words sounded dumb even as they came out of her mouth. The summer *was* long. She wouldn't come back to Virginia until right before school started.

"I wish your dad didn't live so far away, and I wish the summer weren't so long."

"It'll go fast," said Lisa.

"For you, maybe. You'll be in California, surfing or something. I'll just be here, mowing lawns."

"I've never surfed in my life—"

"Until now," said Alex. It was almost a challenge, and Lisa didn't like it.

"I don't want to fight with you," said Lisa.

"I don't want to fight with you, either," he said, relenting. "I'm sorry. It's just that I want things to be different. Not very different. Just a little different."

"Me too," said Lisa. She squeezed his hand. It was a way to keep from saying anything else, because she was afraid that if she tried to speak she might cry, and she hated it when she cried. It made her face red and puffy, but most of all, it told other people how she was feeling. She'd found it useful to keep her feelings to herself these days. Like Alex, she wanted things to be different, but she wanted them to be very different, not just a little. She sighed. That was slightly better than crying.

"I TOLD YOU SO," said Stevie to Callie and Carole.

Stevie had threaded her way through the airport terminal, straight to the cafeteria near the security checkpoint. And there, sitting next to the door, were her twin brother and her best friend.

"Surprise!" the three girls cried, crowding around the table.

"We just couldn't let you be the only one to say goodbye to Lisa," Carole said, sliding into the booth next to Alex.

"We had to be here, too. You understand that, don't you?" Stevie asked Lisa as she sat down next to her.

"And since I was in the car, they brought me along," said Callie, pulling up a chair from a nearby table.

"You guys!" said Lisa, her face lighting up with joy. "I'm so glad you're here. I was afraid I wasn't going to see you for months and months!"

She *was* glad they were there. It wouldn't have felt right if she'd had to leave without seeing them one more time. "I thought you had other things to do."

"We just told you that so we could surprise you. We did surprise you, didn't we?"

"You surprised me," Lisa said, beaming.

"Me too," Alex said dryly. "I'm surprised, too. I really thought I could go for an afternoon, just *one* afternoon of my life, without seeing my twin sister."

Stevie grinned. "Well, there's always tomorrow," she said. "And that's something to look forward to, right?"

"Right," he said, grinning back.

Since she was closest to the outside, Callie went and got sodas for herself, Stevie, and Carole. When she rejoined the group, they were talking about everything in the world except the fact that Lisa was going to be gone for the summer and how much they were all going to miss one another.

She passed the drinks around and sat quietly at the end of the table. There wasn't much for her to say. She didn't really feel as if she belonged there. She wasn't anybody's best friend. It wasn't as if they minded her being there, but she'd come along because Stevie had offered to drive her to a tack shop after they left the airport. She was simply along for the ride.

". . . And don't forget to say hello to Skye."

"Skye? Skye who?" asked Alex.

"Don't pay any attention to him," Lisa said. "He's just jealous."

"You mean because Skye is a movie star?"

"And say hi to your father and the new baby. It must be exciting that you'll meet your sister."

"Well, of course, you've already met her, but now she's crawling, right? It's a whole different thing."

An announcement over the PA system brought their chatter to a sudden halt.

"It's my flight," Lisa said slowly. "They're starting to board and I've got to get through security and then to Gate . . . whatever."

"Fourteen," Alex said. "It comes after Gate Twelve. There are no thirteens in airports."

"Let's go."

"Here, I'll carry that."

"And I'll get this one . . ."

As Callie watched, Lisa hugged Carole and Stevie. Then she kissed Alex. Then she hugged her friends again. Then she turned to Alex.

"I think it's time for us to go," Carole said tactfully.

"Write or call every day," Stevie said.

"It's a promise," said Lisa. "Thanks for coming to the airport. You, too, Callie."

Callie smiled and gave Lisa a quick hug before all the girls backed off from Lisa and Alex.

Lisa waved. Her friends waved and turned to leave her alone with Alex. They were all going to miss her, but the girls had one another. Alex only had his lawns to mow. He needed the last minutes with Lisa.

"See you at home!" Stevie called over her shoulder, but she didn't think Alex heard. His attention was completely focused on one person.

Carole wiped a tear from her eye once they'd rounded a corner. "I'm going to miss her."

"Me too," said Stevie.

Carole turned to Callie. "It must be hard for you to understand," she said.

"Not really," said Callie. "I can tell you three are really close."

"We are," Carole said. "Best friends for a long time. We're practically inseparable." Even to her the words sounded exclusive and uninviting. If Callie noticed, she didn't say anything.

The three girls walked out of the terminal and found their way to Stevie's car. As she turned on the engine, Stevie was aware of an uncomfortable empty feeling. She really didn't like the idea of Lisa's being gone for the summer, and her own unhappiness was not going to be helped by a brother who was going to spend the entire time moping about his missing girlfriend. There had to be something that would make her feel better.

"Say, Carole, do you want to come along with us to the tack shop?" she asked.

"No, I can't," Carole said. "I promised I'd bring in the horses from the paddock before dark, so you can just drop me off at Pine Hollow. Anyway, aren't you due at work in an hour?"

Stevie glanced at her watch. Carole was right. Everything was taking longer than it was supposed to this afternoon.

"Don't worry," Callie said quickly. "We can go to the tack shop another time."

"You don't mind?" Stevie asked.

"No. I don't. Really," said Callie. "I don't want you to be late for work—either of you. If my parents decide to get a pizza for dinner again, I'm going to want it to arrive on time!"

Stevie laughed, but not because she thought anything was very funny. She wasn't about to forget the last time she'd delivered a pizza to Callie's family. In fact, she wished it hadn't happened, but it had. Now she had to find a way to face up to it.

As she pulled out of the airport parking lot, a plane roared overhead, rising into the brooding sky. *Maybe that's Lisa's plane*, she thought. The noise of its flight seemed to mark the beginning of a long summer.

The first splats of rain hit the windshield as Stevie paid their way out of the parking lot. By the time they were on the highway, it was raining hard. The sky had darkened to a steely gray. Streaks of lightning brightened it, only to be followed by thunder that made the girls jump.

The storm had come out of nowhere. Stevie flicked on the windshield wipers and hoped it would go right back to nowhere.

The sky turned almost black as the storm strengthened.

Curtains of rain ripped across the windshield, pounding on the hood and roof of the car. The wipers flicked uselessly at the torrent.

"I hope Fez is okay," said Callie. "He hates thunder, you know."

"I'm not surprised," said Carole, trying to control her voice. It seemed to her that there were a lot of things Fez hated. He was as temperamental as any horse she had ever ridden.

Fez was one of the horses in the paddock. Carole didn't want to upset Callie by telling her that. If she told Callie he'd been turned out, Callie would wonder why he hadn't just been exercised. If she told Callie she'd exercised him, Callie might wonder if he was being overworked. Carole shook her head. What was it about this girl that made Carole so certain that whatever she said, it would be wrong? Why couldn't she say the one thing she really needed to say?

Still, Carole worked at Pine Hollow, and that meant taking care of the horses that were boarding there—and that meant keeping the owners happy.

"I'm sure Fez will be fine. Ben and Max will look after him," Carole said.

"I guess you're right," said Callie. "I know he can be difficult. Of course, you've ridden him, so you know that, too. I mean, that's obvious. But it's spirit, you see. Spirit is the key to an endurance specialist. He's got it, and I think he's got the makings of a champion. We'll work together this summer, and come fall . . . well, you'll see."

Spirit—yes, it was important in a horse. Carole knew

that. She just wished she understood why it was that Fez's spirit was so irritating to her. She'd always thought of herself as someone who'd never met a horse she didn't like. Maybe it was the horse's owner . . .

"Uh-oh," said Stevie, putting her foot gently on the brake. "I think I got it going a little too fast there."

"You've got to watch out for that," Callie said. "My father says the police practically lie in wait for teenage drivers. They love to give us tickets. Well, they certainly had fun with me."

"You got a ticket?" Stevie asked.

"No, I just got a warning, but it was almost worse than a ticket. I was going four miles over the speed limit in our hometown. The policeman stopped me, and when he saw who I was, he just gave me a warning. Dad was furious—at me and at the officer, though he didn't say anything to the officer. He was angry at him because he thought someone would find out and say I'd gotten special treatment! I was only going four miles over the speed limit. Really. Even the officer said that. Well, it would have been easier if I'd gotten a ticket. Instead, I got grounded. Dad won't let me drive for three months. Of course, that's nothing compared to what happened to Scott last year."

"What happened to Scott?" Carole asked, suddenly curious about the driving challenges of the Forester children.

"Well, it's kind of a long story," said Callie. "But—"

"Wow! Look at that!" Stevie interrupted. There was an amazing streak of lightning over the road ahead. The dark afternoon brightened for a minute. Thunder followed instantly.

"Maybe we should pull off the road or something?" Carole suggested.

"I don't think so," said Stevie. She squinted through the windshield. "It's not going to last long. It never does when it rains this hard. We get off at the next exit anyway."

She slowed down some more and turned the wipers up a notch. She followed the car in front of her, keeping a constant eye on the two red spots of the car's taillights. She'd be okay as long as she could see them. The rain pelted the car so loudly that it was hard to talk. Stevie drove on cautiously.

Then, as suddenly as it had started, the rain stopped. Stevie spotted the sign for their exit, signaled, and pulled off to the right and up the ramp. She took a left onto the overpass and followed the road toward Willow Creek.

The sky was as dark as it had been, and there were clues that there had been some rain there, but nothing nearly as hard as the rain they'd left on the interstate. Stevie sighed with relief and switched the windshield wipers to a slower rate.

"I think I'll drop you off at Pine Hollow first," she said, turning onto the road that bordered the stable's property.

Pine Hollow's white fences followed the contour of the road, breaking the open, grassy hillside into a sequence of paddocks and fields. A few horses stood in the fields, swishing their tails. One bucked playfully and ran up a hill, shaking his head to free his mane in the wind. Stevie smiled. Horses always seemed to her the most welcoming sight in the world.

"Then I'll take Callie home," Stevie continued, "and

after that I'll go over to Pizza Manor. I may be a few minutes late for work, but who orders pizza at five o'clock in the afternoon anyway?"

"Now, now," teased Carole. "Is that any way for you to mind your Pizza Manors?"

"Well, at least I have my hat with me," said Stevie. Or did she? She looked into the rearview mirror to see if she could spot it, and when that didn't do any good, she glanced over her shoulder. Callie picked it up and started to hand it to her.

"Here," she said. "We wouldn't want— Wow! I guess the storm isn't over yet!"

The sky had suddenly filled with a brilliant streak of lightning, jagged and pulsating, accompanied by an explosion of thunder.

It startled Stevie. She shrieked and turned her face back to the road. The light was so sudden and so bright that it blinded her for a second. The car swerved. Stevie braked. She clutched at the steering wheel and then realized she couldn't see because the rain was pelting even harder than before. She reached for the wiper control, switching it to its fastest speed.

There was something to her right! She saw something move, but she didn't know what it was.

"Stevie!" Carole cried.

"Look out!" Callie screamed from the backseat.

Stevie swerved to the left on the narrow road, hoping it would be enough. Her answer was a sickening jolt as the car slammed into something solid. The car spun around, smashing against the thing again. When the thing screamed, Stevie knew it was a horse. Then it disappeared from her field of vision. Once again, the car spun. It smashed against the guardrail on the left side of the road and tumbled up and over it as if the rail had never been there.

Down they went, rolling, spinning. Stevie could hear the screams of her friends. She could hear her own voice, echoing in the close confines of the car, answered by the thumps of the car rolling down the hillside into a gully. Suddenly the thumping stopped. The screams were stilled. The engine cut off. The wheels stopped spinning. And all Stevie could hear was the idle *slap, slap slap* of her windshield wipers.

"Carole?" she whispered. "Are you okay?"

"I think so. What about you?" Carole answered.

"Me too. Callie? Are you okay?" Stevie asked.

There was no answer.

"Callie?" Carole echoed.

The only response was the girl's shallow breathing.

How could this have happened?

ABOUT THE AUTHOR

Bonnie Bryant is the author of nearly a hundred books about horses, including The Saddle Club series, Saddle Club Super Editions, and the Pony Tails series. She has also written novels and movie novelizations under her married name, B. B. Hiller.

Ms. Bryant began writing The Saddle Club in 1986. Although she had done some riding before that, she intensified her studies then and found herself learning right along with her characters Stevie, Carole, and Lisa. She claims that they are all much better riders than she is.

Ms. Bryant was born and raised in New York City. She still lives there, in Greenwich Village, with her two sons.

Don't miss Bonnie Bryant's next exciting
Saddle Club adventure . . .

WAGON TRAIL
Saddle Club #81

The Saddle Club is heading west—on the Oregon Trail.
They're taking part in a re-creation of the famous
wagon train ride across the American West. Things may
be a little easier for these modern-day pioneers, but they
still have their fair share of problems, including an obnoxious assistant trail boss and a whiny child. In addition, Stevie has to drive their wagon—and wear a dress!
She isn't sure which is worse. Lisa has to contend with a
reluctant cow that *really* doesn't want to walk across the
prairie. Even Carole is finding the long days in the saddle a little more than she bargained for.

This exciting story continues in *Quarter Horse*, The
Saddle Club #82.

PINE HOLLOW

New Series from Bonnie Bryant

Friends always come first ... don't they?

A lot of new things are happening, but one thing remains the same: Stevie, Lisa, and Carole are still best friends.

Even so, growing up and taking on new responsibilities can be difficult. Now with **high school, driver's licenses, boyfriends,** and **jobs,** they hardly have time for themselves—not to mention each other and their horses!

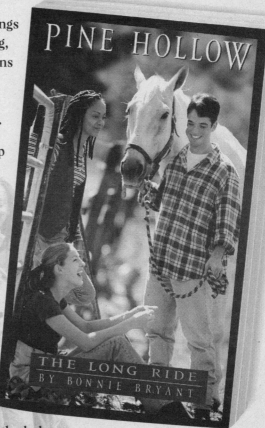

Then an accident leaves a girl's life in the balance, and someone has to take the blame. Can even best friends survive this test?

Coming July 1998 from Bantam Books.